Melanie Fe...
Across Her Cheek,

then his lips on the side of her neck. His words tickled her ears. "We should figure out the sleeping arrangements for tonight."

He rose suddenly and added a couple more logs to the blaze. "There should be some sleeping bags in the cupboard," he said. "And another cot..." It was almost a question.

All right, Ms. I-can-take-care-of-myself-and-don't-need-anybody, what do you plan to do now?

This was not the time to panic, Melanie told herself. She was a self-sufficient woman who would handle this logically and intelligently.

As she watched, Cody jabbed the burning logs, causing embers to fly—like the hot sparks she felt every time he kissed her. The intensity in his face and the captivating pull of his masculinity drew her to him. Her insides melted into a simmering pool of desire.

Maybe common sense and levelheaded thinking weren't all they were cracked up to be....

Dear Reader,

Welcome to Silhouette Desire, where you can discover the answers to *all* your romantic questions. Such as...

Q. *What would you think if you discovered the man you love has a secret identity—as a movie star?*

A. That's what happens to the heroine of August's MAN OF THE MONTH, *Don't Fence Me In* by award-winning writer Kathleen Korbel.

Q. *What would you do if you were pregnant, in labor and snowbound with a sexy—but panicked—stranger?*

A. Discover the answer in *Father on the Brink,* the conclusion to Elizabeth Bevarly's FROM HERE TO PATERNITY series.

Q. *Suppose you had to have a marriage of convenience?*

A. Maybe you'd behave like the heroine in Barbara McMahon's *Bride of a Thousand Days.*

Q. *How could you talk a man into fathering your child...no strings attached?*

A. Learn how in Susan Crosby's *Baby Fever!*

Q. *Would you ever marry a stranger?*

A. You might, if he was the hero of Sara Orwig's *The Bride's Choice.*

Q. *What does it take to lasso a sexy cowboy?*

A. Find out in Shawna Delacorte's *Cowboy Dreaming.*

Silhouette Desire...where all your questions are answered and your romantic dreams can come true.

Until next month, happy reading!

Lucia Macro

Senior Editor

Please address questions and book requests to:
Silhouette Reader Service
U.S.: 3010 Walden Ave., P.O. Box 1325, Buffalo, NY 14269
Canadian: P.O. Box 609, Fort Erie, Ont. L2A 5X3

SHAWNA
DELACORTE
COWBOY DREAMING

SILHOUETTE *Desire*®
Published by Silhouette Books
America's Publisher of Contemporary Romance

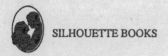

SILHOUETTE BOOKS

ISBN 0-373-76020-5

COWBOY DREAMING

Copyright © 1996 by Sharon K. Dennison

Books by Shawna Delacorte

Silhouette Desire

Sarah and the Stranger #730
The Bargain Bachelor #759
Cassie's Last Goodbye #814
Miracle Baby #905
Cowboy Dreaming #1020

SHAWNA DELACORTE

has sought out new places and experiences after spending most of her life in Southern California. She passed the winter house-sitting in Kansas while her mother and stepfather traveled. Then it was on to the Pacific Northwest and her new home. Even though she now writes full-time, she continues to pursue her interests in photography while traveling to new places and revisiting favorite locations.

Special thanks to my mother and stepfather for
providing me with a calm oasis in the
midst of a hectic year.

One

Melanie Winslow placed her foot on the top step leading to the porch. It creaked as she put her weight on it. *After all these years it still creaks.* Maybe it was the eerie stillness of the night that made the noise seem so much louder than she remembered. Trepidation welled inside her, almost overwhelming the task she had set for herself. She fought the urge to turn and run.

It had been almost ten years since she last stepped foot on the porch of the house where she had lived for the first eighteen years of her life—almost ten years since the day of her mother's funeral. She paused on the front porch and glanced back over her shoulder. The full moon shone brightly in the black sky, casting its silvery glow across the landscape. The crisp night air belied the fact that it was springtime. Melanie shivered inside her jacket, her Southern California clothes not suited to the colder clime.

The pristine whiteness of the fence lined both sides of the long driveway and the plaintive howl of a coyote broke the silence. From the main road the ranch looked more like one of the finest Kentucky Thoroughbred breeding farms than a working cattle ranch in the foothills of eastern Colorado.

She had driven nonstop from Los Angeles and was dead tired. Stifling a yawn, she stood on her toes and reached to the ledge above the front door. She was not sure exactly how she felt when her fingers closed around the key. She had half hoped that it would not be there, that she could turn around and leave, while convincing herself that she had made the effort. She suppressed another yawn. It had been more than thirty hours since she'd had any sleep, not counting a half-hour nap at a roadside rest somewhere in New Mexico when she couldn't keep her eyes open any longer.

Mel inserted the key into the lock and turned it. The dead bolt clicked as it slid back. She placed her hand on the doorknob, then paused and gave another quick look back over her shoulder. Was it too late to turn around, get in her car and start driving back to Los Angeles? She took a calming breath, opened the front door and stepped into the living room.

A dark, shadowy figure lunged at Melanie, knocked the wind from her and shoved her to the floor. She shook her head, momentarily stunned by the force of the blow, then attempted to scramble to her feet. The large body on top of her pinned her to the carpeting. She instinctively struck out at her assailant, digging her fingernails into his bare chest. His strong arms prevented her from putting up much of a fight in her defense. The menacing voice rasped in her ear.

"Stay put unless you want your head bashed in."

Melanie gasped for air, then gasped in terror as a rough hand grazed the side of her neck, brushed across her jacket, then settled over her breast. She knew her voice trembled with fear. It was all she could do to force out the words. "Please . . . don't . . ."

"What the hell—" Shock did not even come close to describing Cody Chandler's reaction to his accidental discovery. He jerked back his hand and jumped to his feet. Moving through the darkness, he flipped on the light switch by the front door.

The intruder lay sprawled on the floor. An oversize jacket covered a body that definitely belonged to a woman—there was no doubt about that fact. Her hazel eyes were wide with fear; her lips slightly parted; her short, dark hair in wild disarray; her legs encased in worn jeans. He felt some of the tension drain away as the adrenaline surge began to wear off.

Melanie gazed up at the large man who loomed over her like some fearful image dredged up from the bottom of her deepest fears. He was dressed in a pair of old jeans and nothing else. With the exception of the hard glint in his blue eyes, he looked as though he had just been roused from sleep. Her pounding heart and racing pulse slowed a bit as her fear subsided.

His tousled blond hair was matted on one side where he had been sleeping on it. She could see the pillow creases on the side of his face. His jeans had been pulled on but only half zipped, and the top snap was open. His hard chest was bare, as were his feet. A bit of calm settled over her as she took in more of his physical attributes.

The scratches she had inflicted on his chest stood out as ugly red marks on skin that showed the beginnings of a golden tan even though it was only April. Wisps of sandy-colored chest hair converged into a narrow line that angled down his stomach and finally disappeared inside his jeans. His shoulders were broad and his arms well muscled. Other than the scar across his right shoulder and the barely discernible bump on his nose where it appeared to have been

broken at one time, he was an incredibly handsome speci-
men of perfect manhood. She guessed his age to be late
thirties.

He made no attempt to help her up from the floor.

"Who the hell are you and what are you doing here?"

He barked out his demands, making it clear exactly who
was in charge.

The fear had passed and the anger set in. Mel scrambled
to her feet, adjusting her disheveled clothing as she regained her balance. Now that she was upright, she realized
just how tall he was, even compared with her five-feet-seven-
inch height. He topped six feet by at least one inch, maybe
even two.

She glared at him defiantly while running her fingers
through her hair in an attempt to untangle it. "How dare
you attack me like that! You're lucky I'm not calling the
police right now."

"*You* calling the police!" He unconsciously rubbed his
fingers across the scratches she had inflicted, then folded his
arms across his chest. "I'm perfectly within my rights to
protect my home against intruders...and other undesir-
ables."

She inwardly bristled at his accusation. She was not sure
which irritated her more, his referring to her as an undesir-
able intruder or his other claim. "*Your* home! No way is this
your home. This house—in fact, this entire ranch and everything on it—belongs to Buck Winslow. I ought to know
because I'm his daughter."

Cody blinked a couple of times and shook his head in an
attempt to clear the sleep. Had he heard correctly? This
woman standing in front of him was Buck Winslow's long-
absent daughter? He never would have recognized her from
the old high-school graduation picture Buck kept by his bed.
Cody finally found his voice and blurted out the first thing

that came to his mind. "You're Melanie Winslow? Where the hell have you been? And why have you bothered to show up after nearly ten years?"

Now it was Mel's turn to be surprised. Just who was this man who seemed to know more about her than a stranger should? "Well, that takes care of who I am. Now, just who are you?"

"I'm Cody Chandler, Buck's ranch foreman."

"Oh, yeah?" *Oh, great—brilliant retort, Mel,* she said to herself. "No way, cowboy. The ranch foreman is Tom Collier, has been for years."

"Not anymore. Arthritis. The doc suggested he might be more comfortable in a warmer, drier climate, so he went to Tucson a little over eight years ago." He fixed her with a cold look. "But, then, you wouldn't know that, would you?"

There was something about the sarcasm in his voice and his aggressive manner that set Melanie's teeth on edge. He seemed just a little too possessive, just a little too much in charge. And where was her father? He had never been a particularly sound sleeper. Surely all the commotion must have been loud enough to wake him. She glanced down the darkened hallway that led to the bedrooms, then turned her attention back to Cody. "Since when does the *hired help* sleep in the main house and refer to the property as theirs? And just where the hell is my father?"

Cody stretched himself to his fullest height. His eyes narrowed and his jaw clenched in a hard line. "You've got quite a mouth on you, kid." He continued to stare at her, refusing to give her any quarter. She certainly did have quite a mouth on her—it was full, lush and very sensual. Just the type of mouth that needed to be kissed—long, hard . . . and often.

"I'm hardly a kid and I certainly don't appreciate your arrogant attitude. Besides, that doesn't answer my question." She adopted a condescending air as she continued to question him. "But if a two-part question is too difficult for you, we can skip the first part and go right to the second." Then, without warning, the hard edge again surrounded her words. "Where is my father? What have you done with him?"

"You weren't concerned a year ago, so why should you be concerned now?" Again he gave her no leeway. He refused to back off or give her any room to maneuver.

The conversation had taken a totally unexpected turn in direction. *Something was wrong...terribly wrong.* The anger drained from Melanie, to be replaced by an unsettling jitter that started in the pit of her stomach and quickly spread throughout her body. Was she too late? Had her decision to resolve the estrangement with her father and attempt to bridge the huge chasm between them come too late? Her voice no longer held the antagonism that had been there just moments earlier. It now told of the new fears that had immediately invaded her consciousness. "A year ago? What happened a year ago?" She swallowed a couple of times in an attempt to put down her rising fear. "What do you mean?"

He instantly caught her change in attitude. Was it possible that she did not know? Had she returned for some reason other than to hover around a dying man in order to be on hand when it came time to cash in on her inheritance? "Buck's been sick for some time now." He weighed his next words carefully as he studied her reaction to what he said. He saw the shock cover her face and a hint of sadness come into her eyes. He was not sure whether to try to cushion the blow of what she apparently did not know, or give her what he believed she deserved by not sparing her feelings.

Mel stumbled backward and plopped into a chair. Her father had been suffering from a lengthy illness? "I...I didn't know." She tried to collect her thoughts. This was not at all what she had expected to find. She had mentally prepared herself for the inevitable string of ongoing arguments with her father, but not for this. She looked up at Cody. "How can this be? He's always been as strong as an ox, never sick a day in his life." She saw it in Cody's eyes. He was not able to hide the deep concern that he felt. "How...what..." Her words trailed off. She was afraid to ask the ultimate question, so she said nothing.

Cody was torn between her genuine surprise and unexpected concern and his resentment of her for the anguish she had put her father—his close friend—through for the past ten years. He steeled himself against the warm spot deep inside that seemed to want to reach out toward her need. "I sent you a letter last June. Since nobody knew how to get in touch with you, I mailed it to the publication that had just printed one of your articles, with a notation for them to forward it to you." Even though he was determined not to make things easy for her, he still inwardly flinched at the bitterness he heard in his words and tone of voice.

Her response was almost a whisper. There was a slight quaver to her voice. "I never received it." She held his steady look for a long moment before she broke eye contact with him. She could see his disapproval, and for some reason it bothered her. That this arrogant, antagonistic, unpleasant stranger seemed to disapprove of her actually *bothered* her. As she glanced away her gaze fell across his taut, well-toned upper torso with the ugly red gouges.

She recaptured his eye contact and he continued to stare at her. His posture and body language still challenged her and her right to have entered the house. She looked away again, and this time her gaze traveled around the living room. It was mostly as she had remembered it with one notable exception. A new recliner occupied a place of honor in the corner, replacing what had been her father's favorite chair.

The old chair had been worn out for as long as Mel could remember. Her mother had bought him a new chair for Christmas one year, but he refused to use it and she had eventually donated it to charity. Apparently the ratty old chair had finally given out and her father had replaced it. Why had he not done it while her mother was still alive? Why had he not shown even the slightest bit of appreciation for her mother's efforts or concern for her mother's feelings? The old hurt flooded into her consciousness. She had thought she was distanced enough from the old memories to be able to handle them. She blinked away the tears.

Cody saw the tears fill her eyes and he wasn't sure what to make of it. He relaxed his stance. "Is something wrong? I didn't hurt you when I knocked you down, did I?"

"No...no, you didn't hurt me. I'm exhausted, that's all. I've driven all the way from Los Angeles without any sleep." She stifled a yawn, as if to reinforce her claim.

She looked in his direction again and gestured toward his bare chest. "In fact, it seems I did the damage to you. I'm sorry."

For the first time Cody noticed the scratches on his chest. It had all happened so quickly he had not been aware of them. The only thing clear in his mind was the moment he had discovered it was a woman he had tackled—the moment his hand closed over her breast. "That's all right. I guess you're entitled to defend yourself, even if you're the one who's the intruder." He had expected some sort of rebuttal from her, but he did not get it.

Mel heard his words but was unable to respond to his accusation. There were too many memories, too many old feelings, all clamoring for her undivided attention. She looked up at Cody again. His stance had softened, as had his expression. "Where's my father?"

"He's moved from his bedroom into the parlor. Not only is it a much larger room, it's also a bright corner room with lots of windows that give him the morning sun. He seems to be more comfortable there. He's asleep now and I don't want him disturbed." Those last words carried the sound of absolute authority, again challenging her right to be there.

"But I'm his daughter—"

"Yes, the daughter who hasn't sent as much as a postcard in nearly ten years." The hard edge returned to Cody's voice as he spoke through clenched teeth. "The daughter who broke his heart."

Mel jumped to her feet. She would not tolerate any more insolence from this stranger who seemed to have appointed himself Lord of the Manor. The angry words spewed out before she could stop them. "How dare you presume to make judgments about me and my relationship with my father? You weren't here. You don't know what happened!" She fought back the tears. Her voice dropped to a mere whisper as she forced the words. "You don't know anything about it." She quickly regained her composure, her indignation once again taking command. "Besides, it's none of your business!" She felt the heat color her cheeks and the angry tears sting her eyes.

The old grandfather clock struck five times, drawing Cody's attention away from Mel. If he were not already standing in the living room, it would be time to get up. He became aware of the cold air against his chest and his bare feet. He did not answer her challenge. He wasn't sure *how* to answer it. Perhaps he had been out of line in what he said, but he certainly had no intention of apologizing. He turned and went to his bedroom to finish dressing.

Mel watched as he walked down the hall and entered the first room on the right, closing the door behind him. Maybe he was through with the conversation, but she was far from finished with him. She charged down the hall and banged open his bedroom door, barging in uninvited. "Hey, you, cowboy—don't you dare turn your back on me and walk away while I'm talking!"

His angry voice matched hers. "And don't you dare—" He didn't bother to finish his sentence, but grabbed her around the waist, effortlessly lifted her off the floor and carried her out into the hallway. Instead of putting her down, he held her up so that they were eye-to-eye, so close their noses were almost touching. His voice was soft, almost a whisper. "And don't you dare barge into my bedroom again unless you have something a lot more interesting on your mind than merely talking." He held her close for a moment longer, then abruptly deposited her on the floor.

He returned to his bedroom and closed the door, leaving Mel in the darkened hallway with her sensibilities totally shaken. She leaned back against the wall for support. What had just happened? One moment she was so angry she could have punched him in the nose and the next moment his nearness literally took her breath away and left her weak in the knees.

Cody peeled off his jeans and tossed them in a corner on his way into his bathroom. He had moved into the main house almost a year ago, when Buck's illness started to take a noticeable physical toll. The bedroom/sitting room/ bathroom suite had originally been for guests, but Buck had insisted that Cody occupy it. The two men had conspired to keep Buck's illness as much of a secret as possible. At the time they were in the process of renegotiating a large existing bank loan being used for expansion and upgrading equipment. Buck didn't want anyone to know he was not running things with his usual iron hand and total authority.

Cody showered, shaved and dressed, but the activity didn't divert him from the nagging memory of his body pressed on top of Melanie's. Her fiery temper had only accentuated the golden sparks that seemed to ignite in her hazel eyes when she lashed out at him with her anger. The lush fullness of her lower lip had trembled slightly when she fought back the tears. Somewhere in the back of his mind he was cognizant of just how much of her physical description had managed to seep into his consciousness. It was a realization that did not please him.

Cody stepped out into the hallway and was greeted by the smell of freshly brewed coffee. It was only five-thirty and the sun was not even up, but already it had been a very eventful morning. He hurried toward the kitchen, telling himself it was the coffee that beckoned rather than the prospect of engaging in another confrontation with Melanie Winslow. He grudgingly admitted to himself that she had done an admirable job holding her ground against him, but he was not sure exactly how he felt about it.

He stopped at the kitchen door. The lights were on, a glass of orange juice sat on the counter and steam rose from the mug of hot coffee beside it, but Melanie was nowhere to be seen.

"Buck." The word escaped his mouth in a hushed urgency as the realization struck him full force. He whirled around and hurried across the house toward the parlor. *If she's disturbed him, I'll*— His thought deserted him as soon as he spotted her standing just inside the parlor door. The expression on her face said it all. The defiant woman he had been sparring with only half an hour ago was gone and in her place stood a lost little girl who looked so in need of someone to take care of her.

Melanie had not been prepared for the sight that greeted her. Her father was six feet four inches tall with a large barrel chest and broad shoulders. He weighed two hundred forty pounds, all of it pure muscle. His hair was jet black and his eyes were a piercing dark brown. All in all, he was quite an imposing sight. At least, that was the way she had remembered him.

The man sleeping in the bed certainly did not fit that description. His hair had thinned considerably and what was left had turned gray. His face was lean, making his squared jaw seem out of proportion. Even in sleep he appeared drawn and haggard. He almost seemed frail—a word she would never in her life have associated with her father. He looked much older than his sixty-four years.

Cody wrapped his strong fingers around her arm and yanked her out of the room. He quietly closed the door before ushering her back to the kitchen. She wrenched her arm out of his grasp and fixed him with an angry stare.

"Just what do you think you're doing? I told you I didn't want Buck disturbed. He needs his rest." He saw the golden flecks ignite in her eyes. The little girl who had been quietly standing at the door of the parlor had vanished and the female wildcat had reappeared. "The last thing he needs is the type of aggravation you represent. Now, stay out of his room. At least until I've had an opportunity to prepare him for this little *surprise.*" Surprise, indeed. That was certainly the biggest understatement of the century.

"I've really had quite enough of this and quite enough of you! Now, get out of my way. I'm going to—"

He grabbed her around the waist and sat her up on the countertop. He leaned in very close to her, as he had done before. "You're going to do exactly what I tell you to do." Cody glanced back over his shoulder toward the kitchen door, then turned toward Mel again. "And try to show a little consideration. Keep your voice down. I don't want your yelling to wake Buck."

As much as Mel hated to agree with this obnoxious bully, he was probably right about waking her father. She might have disagreed with him a little while ago, but as soon as she saw her father she knew Cody had been honest about the condition of his health.

Melanie shoved Cody away and slid off the counter to the floor. She glared at him, hands on hips in as much of a physical challenge as a verbal one. She did make a concerted effort to keep her voice low. "Stop manhandling me as if I were some sort of a round peg you were trying to fit into a square hole."

He laughed. For the first time she actually saw something on his face other than a stern expression or a scowl. It was a nice laugh and an absolutely devastating smile.

"You said it, kid—not me."

Her anger exploded again. "I am not a kid! I'm twenty-eight years old and have traveled in fifteen different countries on five of the seven continents. My photos and articles have appeared in some of the most prestigious and popular magazines in the world. I haven't spent my life stagnating out here—" she waved toward the window in a broad, sweeping gesture "—in the middle of nowhere."

The smile faded from Cody's face. He leveled a cool gaze at her, then spoke in a very controlled voice, showing no emotion. "I'm thirty-seven years old. I have a bachelor's degree in finance and a master's degree in philosophy. I've done my share of world traveling. I'm fluent in both German and French and can get by in Spanish. Now, if we're through comparing résumés perhaps we can return to the problem at hand. Namely, your sudden reappearance—for whatever the reason—and how it can be handled so as not to upset Buck any more than need be."

This man standing in front of her wearing scuffed cowboy boots, worn jeans and a denim work shirt had a master's degree in philosophy and was fluent in both French and German? She hoped her face didn't give her away. Didn't tell him how shocked and at the same time impressed she was with what he had told her. "Well, if those are indeed your credentials, then what are you doing stuck out here in the boonies working on a ranch?"

"I like it here." It was a flat statement that said to one and all that the topic was closed to further discussion. He had been that route before—the society parties, being seen with the right people, only going to the *in* places—and was not interested in traveling over that road again. He wanted his feet planted firmly on real ground, not moving blindly through a world of big-city skyscrapers populated with plastic people.

"Cody?" The voice came from the direction of the parlor. It was not the booming voice of authority it had once been. It grew louder as its owner progressed toward the kitchen. "Is there some problem out there?"

Melanie saw the anger in Cody's eyes and heard the warning in his tone of voice.

"Don't you even hint at the possibility that there might have been the slightest disagreement spoken here this morning. Seeing you is going to be shock enough for Buck without the stress of an unpleasant confrontation."

"Cody—" Buck paused at the kitchen door and blinked several times. He removed his glasses from his shirt pocket and put them on. His expression showed his confusion and uncertainty. His voice was hesitant. "Melanie?" His expression changed as he continued to speak. "Is that you, Mel, honey?"

Cody saw the surprise settle on Buck's face and the shaky movement of his hand as he gripped the doorjamb in an effort to steady himself, and was immediately at his side. He offered Buck a gentle smile as he discreetly cupped his elbow and assisted the older man to the kitchen table without making it appear that the help was needed. "We have an early-morning visitor, Buck. She showed up at the door just a bit ago. Quite a surprise for me. I didn't recognize her from the picture you have."

Buck's face lit up with a warmth Mel had never associated with her father during the entire eighteen years she had lived in the same house with him. His eyes glistened.

"Have you come home, Melanie? Have you finally come home?"

Two

For perhaps the first time in her adult life Melanie Winslow was at a total loss for words. She stole a glance at Cody and caught the stern look he directed toward her. She looked again at her father's deteriorated condition and understood the wisdom of Cody's admonition. Her once hearty and robust father had been reduced to this frail man who appeared at least ten years older than he really was.

"Yes, Father. It's me. I . . ." She swallowed in an attempt to lessen the lump that had begun to form in her throat. She covered her uneasiness by picking up her cup of coffee and carrying it to the table. She sat down across from her father, forcing a smile that she did not really feel. "I just wrapped up an assignment in this area. I . . . I've been working as a photojournalist for several years now and I was shooting a story in Rocky Mountain National Park."

Buck's voice was soft, as if the simple task of talking required an extra effort on his part. "I know all about your work, honey. I've seen your magazine articles." He paused, taking time to catch his breath. "You've done very well for yourself. I'm real proud of you, Mel—we all are." He glanced over at Cody. "Isn't that right?"

"It sure is, Buck." Cody gave his friend a comforting smile as he placed a cup of hot coffee in front of him. "We're all real proud."

To all outward appearances Melanie Winslow and Cody Chandler had been engaged in amiable conversation prior to Buck's arrival. There was nothing in Cody's voice or his expression that would indicate anything to the contrary. Melanie tried her best to be equally diligent in perpetuating the deception, at least until she had a chance to think things through and get a better handle on what was happening.

There would be ample opportunity later for her to let Cody know exactly what she thought about all of this and determine whether she wanted to continue with the charade. First she would need to know exactly what was wrong with her father and the prognosis for his recovery. But for now, she sipped her coffee and tried to pretend that what she had just said was the truth. This was certainly far removed from what she'd had in mind when she started driving from Los Angeles. Actually, she was not sure exactly what she'd had in mind. It was a series of disjointed ideas that had not yet formed into a solid plan.

Melanie was startled out of her thoughts by the feel of a cold hand covering hers—an icy-cold hand. She looked up into the warmth emanating from her father's face. She did not know if it was her imagination, but his color seemed much better than when he first entered the kitchen. There seemed to be a bit of sparkle in his eyes. He did not look as drawn and withered as when she had observed him in his sleep.

She tried not to jerk her hand away but did manage to tactfully withdraw it from his reach. She took another sip of her coffee, her mind frantically trying to produce some sort of basis for polite conversation. "I didn't have an opportunity to see the ranch when I arrived. Even with the full moon it was still too dark. But, from what I could see along the entrance drive, it looks like you've made several changes."

"You can credit Cody with that." Buck glanced over at his friend and ranch foreman. The genuine affection he felt for the man was obvious. "He's really been an asset. I'm afraid the place was getting a little run-down. Then Cody came on the scene and things really turned around. Now it's quite a showplace in addition to being a model of efficiency. We've almost doubled our productivity and increased our profit margin substantially. It's really something to be proud of."

"Well, that's nice." She heard the strain in her voice and wished she had better control of it.

"You're going to be real surprised by what you see, honey." He continued, then stopped as if a thought had struck him. "Are you all settled in okay? Did you put your things in your old bedroom? I've kept it for you, honey, just the way you left it." Again he reached across the table and covered her hand with his in a loving gesture. "I knew you'd come back home someday."

Cody noticed the grimace that crossed her face at the mention of the ranch being her home and the way her body stiffened when Buck covered her hand. He felt his insides tighten. He did not have time for this nonsense—catering to Buck's wayward daughter. As far as he was concerned, she could get back into her car and head west until she reached the ocean. The only thing that kept him from telling her to do just that was his very real affection for Buck and his concern for the old man's health. She seemed to be having a positive effect on him.

"No, I haven't unpacked yet. My things are still in the car."

Buck twisted around in his chair until he faced Cody. "Would you bring in Mel's things for me and put them in her room?"

"Sure thing, Buck." *Move the little ingrate into the house, as though I have nothing better to do.*

"And, Cody, as soon as we finish breakfast, why don't you take Mel and show her around the ranch? Reacquaint her with her home," Buck suggested.

Cody glanced at the wall clock. It would be sunrise very soon now. The ranch hands would have finished breakfast and started on the day's work. Now that the snow had disappeared from all but the highest elevations of the ranch property, there were fences to mend and outbuildings to be checked. Spring also meant roundup, which created lots of extra work. He really did not have the time to spare, but if that was what it took to keep her from upsetting Buck, then that was what he would do. "Sure thing, boss."

Melanie could see it in Cody's face. He was no more happy with the prospect of giving her a guided tour than she was of having him do it. It would, however, allow them the opportunity to talk in private so she could gather some information and they could get a few things settled between them. Beyond that, she had no thoughts about what she would do or any clear-cut plans for the future.

"I'll start something for breakfast." It was not the type of thing Mel would normally have volunteered for, but anything was better than sitting at the table trying to think of something pleasant to say. She opened the refrigerator door and stared at the contents. She may have been accomplished at many things, but cooking was not one of them.

Since she was out on assignment more often than she was home she usually ate in restaurants. When she was home, opening a carton of yogurt and making coffee for breakfast or popping a frozen entrée into the microwave or having pizza delivered for dinner were about the most difficult cooking tasks she ever attempted.

"You don't need to bother." Cody reached past her, placed his hand on the refrigerator door and shoved it closed. "Edna will be here in a few minutes. She'll take care of making breakfast."

"Edna?" Cody's arm had actually brushed against her shoulder when he leaned past her. He smelled of soap and mint mouthwash. The memory of his body covering hers on the living-room floor was still very fresh in her mind.

"Edna Powers is our cook and housekeeper."

Buck's voice interrupted her thoughts about Cody.

"She's worked for me for almost ten years, ever since..." His voice, not strong at best, trailed off as the emotion clouded his face and choked his words. "Ever...ever since I lost your mother and you."

It's a real pity you wouldn't hire some help before my mother worked herself to death. Maybe if you had she'd still be alive today. The words had popped into her head, uninvited and too strident even to Mel's own ears.

Cody watched her face contort in anger. A glance at the other side of the table told him that Buck had not noticed. He wondered what was going through her mind. Exactly what had happened between Buck and his daughter? He had never really understood why Melanie Winslow left home and left her father at a time when he most needed the closeness of family, especially his only child. Buck had said very little about it and had never uttered a harsh word about his daughter.

"Where's your stuff? In the trunk of your car?" Cody held out his hand toward Mel. "Give me your car keys."

She quickly jumped to her feet. "I'll help you. I have my camera equipment and notebook computer as well as my luggage." She was not yet ready to be alone with her father. Everything she had anticipated and prepared for had refused to materialize. This man was very far removed from the cold, unfeeling monster of a person she had carried in her memory for all these years—*that* man she had been prepared to do battle with. But now that she saw him . . .

She followed Cody out of the house. When they reached the front porch, he came to an abrupt halt and whirled around. Melanie bumped into him before she could stop herself. His rock-hard body made it seem as if she'd run into a stone wall. He grabbed her shoulders to keep her from falling at the same moment that she put her hands against his chest to steady her balance. Even though she wanted to believe it was so, she knew it was more than the accidental collision that had knocked the breath from her. Once again his body was pressed against hers. Once again she felt the stimulating warmth caused by his touch.

"Camera . . . notebook computer . . . luggage." He released his hold on her and took a step back, wanting to put a little distance between them. He had not intended for them to come into physical contact again, at least not like this and certainly not here and now. "Does this mean you plan to stay for a while?"

She also took a step back, putting even more distance between them. "I don't know. I guess I hadn't really thought that far in advance." She found his nearness to be irritating, uncomfortable, very disconcerting—and almost unbearably exciting.

"You must have had something in mind when you showed up here. You claim you didn't know about Buck's health, so that must not be the reason." He furrowed his brow as he folded his arms across his chest. "Just what is it you want? Why are you here?"

The gray predawn sky was giving way to streaks of red and gold. The chilly early-morning air cut through her lightweight jacket, causing a shiver to crawl across her skin. Perhaps staying in the kitchen with her father would have been preferable after all. She pulled together more composure than she actually felt. "I don't owe you any explanations. Now, are you going to help me with my things or do I need to do it myself?" Well, that said it all. Whether it had been her original intention or not, she had just committed to staying at least until the next day.

"Okay, you win this round. But we're not through with this yet." He fixed her with a hard stare. "I won't allow you to upset Buck. Until I know what your game is, I'll be watching your every move. All you have to do is look over your shoulder and you'll find me."

He unfolded his arms and turned toward her car. He was not through with Melanie Winslow, not by a long shot. To create a scene right now would only upset Buck, and that was the last thing Cody wanted to do. He had noticed the way Buck's color had improved, the way his physical condition seemed to perk up around his daughter.

Neither of them spoke as they unloaded the car and carried her belongings into the house. She preceded him down the hallway toward her old bedroom. She reached out for the doorknob, then hesitated as the sinking feeling settled in the pit of her stomach. What in the name of all that was rational and logical was she doing? When had she lost control of what was happening? How had things suddenly become so twisted around that her overbearing father once again had control of her decisions?

Cody noted the hesitation in her actions, then the frantic look on her face when she turned toward him. He cocked his head and raised an eyebrow in a questioning manner. "What's the matter? Did you leave something in the car?"

"Uh, no, I have everything." She gathered her courage, opened the bedroom door, flipped on the light switch and stepped three paces inside the room before stopping.

Her gaze traveled around the bedroom, quickly taking in the entire scene, then returning to do a more thorough appraisal. It was just as she had left it. Obviously it had been cleaned on a regular basis, but the same bedspread lay on the bed and the same curtains covered the windows. Her early efforts at photography were still framed and hanging on the walls. Her bookcase still held her schoolbooks. The picture of her mother still rested on the nightstand. A wrenching tightness knotted in the pit of her stomach. All the old memories, all the old feelings—

"Are you going to stand there forever?"

Cody's interruption startled her. She spun around to face him. "I . . . it's been a long time . . ."

He saw it on her face and in her eyes. It was certainly not what he had expected. It was not the hard, defiant edge of a tough woman that she had tried to project since her arrival. Once again he saw the same little girl who had stood just inside the door of the parlor, looking so confused and in need of comfort.

"Would you rather stay in another room?" He didn't know exactly where the question had come from. It just sort of popped out of his mouth. He certainly hadn't been aware of any conscious desire to make things easier for her—not this woman who had caused his good friend so much despair and hurt.

Mel only half heard his question. She walked across the room to the nightstand, set her notebook computer and camera bag on the bed, then picked up the photograph of her mother. She had left the house so quickly that she had packed only one suitcase with the basic necessities and nothing else. When she realized that she had not packed the photograph of her mother she had almost gone back to get it . . . almost. She'd had to make do with the picture she carried in her memory and in her heart.

Cody carried her three suitcases into the room and placed them next to the closet. He certainly recognized the picture she was holding. It was the same photograph Buck had next to his bed, along with Melanie's high-school graduation picture. He had not seen it so much then, not from the comparison of two photographs, but now he realized just how much Melanie looked like her mother. He wanted to say something to her, but didn't know what to say.

Cody left the bedroom, left Melanie alone with her thoughts and memories, and returned to the kitchen. Edna had arrived and was busy fixing breakfast while Buck sat at the table. Cody poured himself a cup of coffee and sat down across from Buck.

Edna was a pleasant woman, about sixty years old. She always had a warm smile and a cheery word. Buck had hired her within two weeks of the double tragedy of losing both his wife and daughter. She had been a real blessing to the daily activities of the ranch. Nothing seemed to bother her. She took all emergencies in stride right along with her regular duties. It was through Edna, a little over a year later, that Cody had come to work for Buck.

Buck removed the pack of cigarettes from his pocket, but before he could light one Cody took it away from him. "You know what the doctor said about these."

"You don't really think these things could do me any more harm than has already been done, do you?" Buck picked up the cigarette, stared at it for a moment, heaved a sigh of resignation, then put it back in the pack.

"Breakfast is ready." Edna set a plate in front of Buck and another one in front of Cody. "Now, you eat while it's good and hot."

Buck stared at the amount of food on his plate. "What are you trying to do to me, Edna? Look at all of this—eggs, bacon, hash browns, biscuits and gravy—there's enough here to feed an army. I'll never be able to eat all of this."

"You just try your best. I mean to put some meat back on those bones of yours. Lord knows you don't eat enough to keep a fly going."

Buck drank his orange juice, crunched on a strip of bacon and ate a bite of scrambled eggs before turning his attention back to Cody. "Well, you haven't said anything. What do you think?"

Cody took a swallow of his coffee before answering. He knew what Buck was talking about and didn't really want to get involved in the conversation. "Think about what?"

"You know...about Melanie." Buck's face clearly displayed the fatherly pride he felt. "Isn't she about the prettiest little thing you've ever laid eyes on?"

"Sure, Buck. She's very attractive." Cody quickly took a bite of toast, then added a forkful of eggs in order to discourage any further conversation. He had tried his best to sound neutral, to express neither enthusiasm nor displeasure. He went over the words in his mind, the edge of sarcasm attaching itself in spite of his good intentions. *Sure, Buck. She's very attractive.*

He washed the food down with another large swallow of black coffee, not at all happy with the conflicting thoughts and feelings that suddenly flooded his consciousness. *Absolutely, Buck. Very attractive, Buck. Even with tangled hair, rumpled clothes, no sleep and a surly enough attitude*

*to keep most people at bay she still would have no trouble
at all in capturing any man's attention... at least, she sure
captured mine.*

"I've moved my things into my... into *the* bedroom."

Cody looked up at the sound of Melanie's voice. She had
removed her jacket, run a brush through her hair and added
a touch of color to her lips. His gaze traced the curve of her
hip and the swell of her breast beneath the soft sweater she
wore, a swell he had almost come to know intimately. *Ah,
yes... she's very attractive, Buck. That, she is.* His brow
inadvertently furrowed into a frown. *Very attractive, indeed... dammit.* He took another sip of his coffee, hoping
it would somehow wash away his totally unacceptable
thoughts.

"Come on, Mel, honey. Sit down and have some breakfast." Buck turned his attention toward Edna, his face
beaming with delight. "Edna, I'd like you to meet my
daughter. This is Melanie." He gazed lovingly at his daughter as he continued to talk. "She's finally come back home."

The discomfort was almost more than Melanie could
bear. The expression on his face, the warmth in his
voice... this man was a stranger to her, not the father she had
known when she was growing up. She looked toward the
woman standing at the stove. Melanie offered her a smile.
"Hello, Edna. It's nice to meet you."

"It's nice to finally meet you, too. Buck has mentioned
you so many times." Edna gathered another place setting
and carried it to the table. "You come make yourself comfortable and I'll have your breakfast ready for you in just a
minute."

"Please don't go to any trouble. Just some juice and coffee will be fine." Mel noted the amount of food on both
Buck's and Cody's plates and spoke up quickly before Edna

had a chance to start cooking more. "I'm really not much of a breakfast person."

"Nonsense. There's lots of hard work to ranching and everyone needs a big, hot breakfast."

Like it or not, Melanie ended up with a plate full of food. She surprised herself by eating most of it. Once the first bite was in her mouth she realized she was as hungry as she was tired. It had been a long time since her hamburger at a fast-food place late yesterday afternoon.

When she finished breakfast Melanie pushed back from the table and stood. "If you'll excuse me, I think I'll take a walk—get some fresh air. I'm not accustomed to eating a big breakfast." She offered a weak smile to both her father and Cody. "All that food, added to the fact that I haven't had any sleep...I'm not sure how long I'll be able to keep my eyes open." It was the truth, as far as it went. What she had not said was how uncomfortable her father's conversation made her feel.

All through breakfast he kept talking about how happy he was that she had finally come home. *Come home*...the words rang hollow in her ears. This was not her home. It may have been where she had lived for her first eighteen years, but it was not her home. She pursed her lips and furrowed her brow as a thought passed through her mind. Exactly where was her home? It seemed that she spent as much time on the road as she did in her apartment. There was no real feeling of permanency to her life, no solid foundation to draw strength and comfort from in troubled times.

She stepped out onto the front porch and looked across the landscape. The hillsides were carpeted in an emerald velvet dotted with patches of brightly colored wildflowers, signaling the end of winter. The breeze rustled through the new leaves on the trees, creating a background whisper that softened the harsh sounds of the squawking blue jays. She shielded her eyes from the bright morning sun and watched as a hawk circled overhead. The crisp, cool air filled her lungs, the sweet smells of spring tickling her senses. How different it was from the choking fumes of car exhaust and the congestion of the Los Angeles freeways.

She left the porch and started down the path toward the barn. As a child the barn had been her place of refuge, the safe haven where she could hide from everything and everyone. She had created an entire imaginary world for herself up in the hayloft. She was the beautiful princess in her castle, waiting for a handsome prince to come along and sweep her up onto his horse and ride away with her.

She opened the barn door and stepped into the dimly lit interior. The barn was empty. She knew the ranch hands would have been hard at work from the first light of day. The barnyard chores would already have been done—the cows milked, chickens fed, eggs collected. She climbed the ladder to the loft, found a soft spot and snuggled into the hay. Her eyelids fluttered shut and within a few seconds she had fallen asleep, visions of a handsome prince dancing through her mind. A handsome prince who bore a remarkable resemblance to Cody Chandler.

"I can handle this, Cody." It had only been during the past year, when his health dictated that he spend more and more time in the office rather than out on the ranch, that Buck had finally learned how to use the computer. Now he took care of all the office functions, including the daily bookkeeping chores, leaving the heavy-duty accounting to Cody and their CPA. Up until a year ago Cody had handled the entire business end of things, but now he had to take up the outdoor slack left by Buck's diminished capacity.

"You've really come a long way with that computer."

"Yeah, it just goes to show...you really can teach an old dog new tricks." Buck swiveled around in his chair until he faced Cody. "I haven't seen Melanie since she left the table after breakfast." He checked his watch. "That was over three hours ago. I know there's lots of work to be done, what with us coming up on spring roundup, but could you check on her? Make sure she's okay? Maybe show her around the ranch and point out the improvements we've made in the past few years?"

"Sure thing, Buck. I was about to head outside anyway." He felt the irritation again. But was it irritation at being expected to look after her or did it go deeper than that? Was he really irritated by the fact that she had not strayed very far from his thoughts since the moment he flipped on the living-room light and saw her sprawled on the floor?

Cody had no idea where she had disappeared to. He checked down the hallway, but she was not in her bedroom. He asked Edna, who said she had not seen Melanie since she had noticed her through the kitchen window going into the barn, but that had been quite a while ago. He left the house and headed toward the barn. It gave him a place to start looking.

It didn't take long for Cody to discover Melanie's whereabouts. He stood on the top rung of the ladder leading to the hayloft and watched her as she slept. The sunlight streamed in through the open loft doors, covering her face in a golden glow. Her features showed no signs of her earlier anger. Her long, dark lashes rested against her upper cheek. Pieces of straw were tucked into the folds of her hair. Her breasts slowly rose and fell with her breathing. *Yes, indeed, she's very attractive....*

Cody climbed up the last step into the loft, though he wasn't exactly sure why, and stood for a moment, staring down at her. Then he knelt next to her sleeping body. He carefully plucked a piece of straw from her hair and gently tickled the tip of it across her cheek. She stirred but did not wake as she batted her hand at the intrusion. He withdrew for a moment, then traced her lower lip with the straw. That tempting mouth—that very tempting mouth—still begged to be kissed. It was a temptation he could not resist. He bent over her, lowering his head until their mouths were within a fraction of an inch. He hesitated, then brushed his lips against hers.

It was the most delicious dream. In fact, it seemed almost real to Melanie. The handsome prince of her childhood fantasies had come for her. She felt his lips against hers, felt the heat and passion of his kiss, even though it only lasted a fraction of a second. She slowly opened her eyes and dreamily focused on Cody's face. He seemed so real, as if she could actually reach out and touch him. She lifted her hand and extended it toward him. Then the dream ceased to be. Reality presented itself as her fingers came in contact with a flesh-and-blood man.

Melanie jerked upright, her eyes wide with shock. Her voice trembled; her words came out in a hushed gasp. "What do you think you're doing?"

Three

———

It was a valid question, but Cody did not have a good answer. He was not sure exactly what he thought he was doing, or more accurately *why* he was doing it. There was nothing about Melanie Winslow that said she was in any way the type of woman with whom he would want to pursue a serious relationship. She was also Buck's daughter and Buck was not only his friend, Buck was his employer. But still, like it or not, something other than her good looks had worked its way under his skin.

He wanted to push it aside as being a ridiculous thought that had no place in his world. He tried, but was not totally successful. He decided to ignore her question. "If you wanted to take a nap shouldn't you be doing it in your bedroom rather than up here?"

Melanie was not sure exactly what had been real and what had been a dream. Had he really kissed her? Perhaps the best thing would be to proceed as if nothing had happened.

She sat up, carefully avoiding any physical contact with him. A hint of embarrassment found its way into her voice. "I didn't mean to fall asleep. I used to come up here when I was a little girl. I guess I . . ." She could not finish her sentence. She did not have a ready explanation for her actions. "What time is it? How long have I been sleeping?"

Cody stood up and reached out his hand to help her to her feet. "It's been about four hours since you left the kitchen."

"Four hours? Oh, no. I certainly didn't intend to be out here that long." She hesitated a moment, then accepted his assistance. "I guess I was just too tired to keep my eyes open." She noticed the way he kept staring at her, a stare that caused a ripple of confusion and vexation in her. She was also very much aware that he still held her hand within his grasp. She quickly withdrew from his touch and busied herself straightening her clothes and brushing away the loose pieces of hay.

Cody pulled several pieces of straw from her hair. He tickled the last piece across her cheek before dropping it to the floor of the hayloft. It was a brief moment of peaceful coexistence, neither challenging the other's position or authority.

It was Melanie who broke the moment. She shifted her weight uncomfortably from one foot to the other as she stared down at the hay-covered floor. She nervously cleared her throat, then looked up at him. "I, uh, I think I owe you an apology. I guess I was a little overly tired this morning. I'm afraid I wasn't too polite."

"Well . . ." An apology—that was certainly far removed from what he had anticipated. Perhaps Buck's daughter was not quite the disagreeable ingrate Cody had surmised her to be. "I certainly can't blame you for getting upset about being tackled and thrown to the floor."

"And I hadn't let anyone know I would be arriving in the middle of the night. I can understand why you would assume I was someone breaking into the house." She stuck out her hand and offered him a tentative smile. "Truce?"

Cody hesitantly agreed, still a little skeptical about her real motives. He accepted her handshake, the sensation of her touch sending a hint of both alarm and anxiety through his awareness. "Sure...truce."

This time it was Cody who quickly withdrew his hand. He ran it across the back of his neck. For a moment he had forgotten his purpose in being there, had forgotten about everything except the mystery and allure of Melanie Winslow. "Shall we go?" He turned toward the ladder. "Buck wants me to show you around, point out everything new over the past ten years." He could not stop the irritation that crept into his voice. It was a silly waste of his time. She had lived at the ranch and should be able to spot the changes on her own without taking up his valuable time.

Her manner stiffened. She wrinkled her brow into a slight frown and pursed her lips. She caught the edge to his voice. Was this part of his method of keeping a vigilant eye on her, as he had threatened? "I don't need a tour guide to find my way around."

He paused with his foot on the top rung of the ladder. His voice and physical presence carried absolute authority. "Buck wants me to show you around, so that's what I'm going to do."

Her temper flared. "This is ridiculous! I lived here for eighteen years. I'll bet I know places on this ranch you've never seen."

He matched her, word for angry word, as he stepped back onto the loft floor. "Look, kid. There've been lots of changes around here in the past ten years. Things are very busy right now. I don't want you wandering around on your own and getting in the way. Besides, I still don't know what you're doing here and until I do—''

She stomped over to the ladder. ''Get out of my way, cowboy.'' She expertly sidestepped him and quickly descended the ladder. She glanced back up when she reached the dirt floor of the barn. He appeared as a large, dark silhouette against the brilliant blue sky visible through the opened loft doors behind him.

''Humph!'' She snorted her indignation, turned on her heel and stormed out of the barn, comforting herself with the knowledge that she had tried to make amends. She had apologized to him, even though she knew she had not been at fault, and had called for a truce. She certainly would not accept any responsibility for the behavior of such an overbearing jerk. A little tremor darted through her body as she recalled her dream, the dream that had seemed so real.

Cody watched from the loft doors as she headed back toward the house. Her stride was purposeful and direct, each step hitting the ground with a thud that he imagined he could almost hear. Then the thought hit him. He glanced at his watch. He needed to hurry if he was going to prevent her from disturbing Buck.

A couple of months ago Buck started taking a short nap before lunch. The short nap had gradually become longer and longer, then became a midmorning nap, an afternoon nap and an evening nap. There was no reason for him to continue to get up as early as he did. Cody had tried to get him to sleep later in the morning, but to no avail. Cody had not belabored the point. Buck had spent his entire life rising before dawn.

Cody understood Buck's need to feel that he was still capable of making a contribution to the daily work effort. For a man like Buck Winslow to be denied his feeling of usefulness was tantamount to denying him a reason to go on liv-

ing. And Cody wanted to do everything he possibly could to
see to it that Buck would be around for as long as possible.
He flashed on the unexpected way Buck had seemed to perk
up around his daughter. The thought left as quickly as it had
arrived. Cody climbed down from the hayloft and hurried
toward the house. He went straight to the office, irritation
growing inside him to the point where it shoved aside whatever tender feelings he might have momentarily harbored
toward Melanie.

Melanie again found herself watching her father as he
slept, only this time he was stretched out in the recliner in the
living room. The nap she had stolen in the hayloft had
somewhat cleared the fuzziness from her sleep-deprived
brain. She needed to dig out some straight answers. Exactly what was wrong with her father and what involvement and authority did this Cody Chandler person have in
her father's business affairs? He projected an air of authority far beyond that of hired hand, even that of ranch
foreman.

She could not imagine her father as either weak or vulnerable. He had always been in charge of everything around
him. Nothing happened on the ranch that he did not know
about. She remembered him as an unemotional, pragmatic
man. The ranch had always come first in his life. He had
been fair with his employees, but his family was a different
matter. She had been hurt on more than one occasion when
he had turned his back on her and walked away when she
had tried to talk to him. He had never allowed any tenderness or softness to show through. If that side of him existed
at all, she had never been aware of it. But seeing him
now... again she was struck by how frail he appeared. Was
Cody Chandler nothing more than an opportunist taking
advantage of a sick man?

Melanie Winslow was confused. Very confused. For some unknown reason she found herself experiencing the very foreign sensation of feeling protective toward her father—protective of this cold, overbearing man with whom she had a relationship that could be described at best as adversarial.

She shook her head to clear the strange thoughts. Sleep. She needed more sleep. Obviously she was not thinking clearly. She turned around and left the living room. She would find Cody Chandler and get some answers from him. Then she would put a call in to Henry Sanderson.

Henry had been Buck's attorney for more years than Melanie was old. She furrowed her brow in thought. That is, assuming Henry was still her father's attorney. It was possible that he, too, was no longer connected with the ranch or her father, just as Tom Collier was no longer on the scene.

Was this all some sort of plot engineered by Cody so that he could get his hands on her father's ranch? Was he really some sort of slick con man? *Good grief! Get a grip on yourself, Melanie. Next you're going to be imagining subterfuge behind every rock and tree.* She tried to put her thoughts into some sort of logical reality. Her father was obviously in bad health and not capable of performing the hard work connected with a large cattle ranch. It was necessary for him to delegate a lot of the authority and responsibility. Even without the tour that Cody seemed determined to give her she could see that there had been lots of changes since she was last there. Things looked very prosperous.

Melanie turned to leave the living room and immediately ran into Cody in the hallway leading from the office. She fixed him with a determined stare, refusing to give credence to the tremor of excitement caused by his presence. "I want a word with you."

He folded his arms across his chest and carefully scrutinized her stance and her physical challenge. He took his time answering her, noting the way she kept clenching and unclenching her jaw. "I thought we were already having words."

She refused to be put off by his aggressive manner. "So far those words have consisted of you barking orders. Now it's time for you to start answering some questions."

He stepped aside and made a sweeping gesture with his arm, indicating the front door. "Outside." It was only one word, but it was said with total authority—once again he was issuing orders.

She hesitated for a moment, glanced back at her father sleeping peacefully in his recliner, then walked out onto the front porch.

Cody leaned back against the porch railing and tucked his hands into his jeans pockets. He studied her nervousness for a moment before speaking. "All right, what do you want answered?"

"First, I want to know about my father's health." Some of the antagonistic edge disappeared from her voice as her inner fears seeped through. "How bad is he?"

"He's dying." The words were said in a flat tone of voice as Cody made every effort to control the emotion welling inside him.

Mel blinked a couple of times, then swallowed quickly several times as she tried to force down the sick feeling. "What..." She gulped in some cool air. "What do you mean?"

"I mean exactly what I said—he's dying. What part of that don't you understand?" He was fully aware of the harshness of his words but did not seem to be able to say it any other way. He had already been through it all with Buck—the anger, the denial and the eventual acceptance. It had been a year ago that the physical deterioration began to take its toll and Cody had written the letter to Buck's daughter. And now here she was, a year later, making demands as if she actually had some sort of concern or involvement.

She stumbled backward, the shock of Cody's words hitting her as sharply as if he had reached out and slapped her. She had seen with her own eyes how her father had been reduced to a shell of his former self. Somewhere deep in her subconscious she had suspected the truth, but she had not been prepared for the reality to hit her so abruptly. Was this how it would end? Would her relationship with her father remain unresolved? For a fraction of a second it was herself she felt sorry for—for the possibility that she might have waited too long and was now too late to change things.

"What...when..." She tried to force a calm to her words. "How much time does he have? What is he dying of?"

Her genuine shock and obvious sorrow managed to pierce the wall Cody had purposely constructed between himself and this woman, of whom he disapproved yet at the same time found very enticing. He steeled himself against the emotional pull that reached out from her and tried to take hold of him.

"As to when, the doctor says he's already on borrowed time. In fact, he said Buck should have been bedridden a couple of weeks ago." He saw the color drain from her face and the unsteady manner in which she reached out to grab hold of the porch railing. He heard her ragged intake of breath.

"Doc says he honestly doesn't know what's kept Buck going." Cody recalled the warmth that covered Buck when he first saw Melanie in the kitchen, some sort of inner peace separate from his acceptance of his mortality. A hint of cognizance tried to push its way into his mind, a thought that said perhaps it was the farfetched hope of a reunion with his daughter that had kept Buck going against all odds.

Cody doubled his resolve to keep control of the situation. He did not know why Melanie Winslow had decided to show up at this particular time, but he was determined to keep her from doing anything to spoil things. He wanted Buck's final days to be as carefree and comfortable as possible.

"And...what...is he in much pain?" Melanie did not know what she felt; she mostly just felt numb. "Shouldn't he be in the hospital?"

"Doc Gerrard doesn't feel there is anything that can be done for him in the hospital that can't be done here at home. This is where Buck wants to be. This is where he's the most comfortable. This is where he has spent his life and where he wants to die. The pain is pretty much controlled by medication. Some days are better than others, but in the past couple of months he's gone downhill rapidly. He's a fighter. He's accepted that he's dying, but he hasn't given up yet. Something is keeping him going, but I don't know..." His voice trailed off as the thought forced its way into his mind again. Was it possible that Buck had found the will to push himself forward in an all-out effort to hang on to life in the hope of seeing his daughter again?

Cody took a calming breath. He did not like talking about it but knew she had to be told the truth. "The what is a little more complex. What he's dying from is cancer, but during the past few years he's been plagued by several other ailments and problems, not the least of which is poor circulation. It's only through sheer will that he's still getting around at all, let alone unassisted. His legs can't hold out much longer. You felt his touch, how cold his skin feels."

"But can he get proper medical care out here, so far away from a major hospital?" Her mind tried desperately to take hold and fully comprehend all she had heard.

"The doc stops by once a week. There's a hospice nurse who comes by three times a week, and there's Edna, of course. Edna has experience along these lines. Her husband died in much the same manner. It was right after that that she came to work for Buck. She keeps a very close eye on him during the day. I've tried to hire a private nurse for twenty-four-hour coverage, but Buck won't have it."

"But in case of an emergency..."

"He can be helicoptered to the hospital in twenty minutes."

Melanie fell back against the wall and stared blankly at the ground as she tried to assimilate everything Cody had told her. A sick feeling churned in the pit of her stomach.

"Are you all right?" Cody's genuine concern showed in his voice as he reached out to give her some support. He cocked his head and studied her for a moment. She was still ashen and visibly shaken, but making a valiant effort to remain calm.

Melanie felt momentarily light-headed. Then she felt his fingers close around her arm and her body being drawn against his. His strong arms were around her a moment later. Cody had stated all the horrible particulars of her father's illness in such a matter-of-fact way, almost as if he were reciting a grocery list. But she knew she could not fault him. He clearly had a genuine concern for Buck's comfort and well-being. She had noticed it in his eyes and had heard it in his warnings to her about upsetting her father.

"I see." She looked up at him, attempting to regain some sort of control over the conversation. There were too many conflicting emotions...the stark reality of her father's health and the equally real sensation of the warmth of Cody's embrace. She saw a moment of tenderness flicker across his face when their eyes locked for a heated instant. She recalled the vivid dream where he had brushed his lips against hers. Too many conflicts...too much confusion. Nothing was happening the way she had anticipated.

This was not right, Melanie told herself. She had to extract herself from the very personal moment they were sharing. She could not deny her attraction to Cody, but she did not know exactly what his game was, and until she had him figured out she needed to keep her distance. She did not trust him...at least not yet. She also questioned whether she could trust herself where Cody Chandler was concerned.

He exerted no physical pressure on her. As soon as she pushed back from him, he released his hold on her. She nervously ran her fingers through her hair. "Uh, does my father know everything?"

"I would never keep anything from him. He's not the type of man who would want to hide from the truth or be shielded from reality. You're his daughter—you should know that. He prefers to meet things head-on and deal with them straight out." He liked the way she had felt in his arms. It had been warm and comfortable—there was no denying that. It was the type of feeling that said there should be more, but until he figured out exactly why she had shown up when she had, he needed to keep a wary eye on her. "Buck knows everything."

"I wouldn't go so far as to say I know *everything*. I did miss the final 'Jeopardy' question on television yesterday." Buck pushed open the screen door and moved unsteadily out onto the front porch, a slight grin playing at the corners of his mouth. "Is it possible that I've been the topic of conversation? It would seem to me that two attractive young people could find something better to do on a beautiful spring day than discuss the accumulated knowledge of this old man.''

Melanie caught the warning look Cody shot her way. She turned toward her father. "Sixty-four isn't very old... Father." She could not call him "Daddy," as she had when she was a little girl. The word was totally out of place. It had a feel of warmth, closeness and familiarity that she did not associate with her father.

"Has Cody been taking care of you, Melanie?"

Taking care of her? The sensation of being wrapped in Cody's embrace immediately leaped to mind. What had her father meant by that comment? Had he seen them? She stole an embarrassed glance in Cody's direction.

Cody did his best to suppress the devilish grin that tugged at the corners of his mouth as he watched her discomfort. Regardless of how innocent Buck's comment might have been, Cody could not help the thought that taking care of her might not be that bad an idea.

Buck seemed oblivious to his faux pas. "What do you think about all the improvements?"

"Actually, Buck..." Cody quickly stepped in to take charge of the conversation. "I haven't had a chance to give her a tour yet. We were discussing doing just that as soon as we finished lunch."

"It's my fault, Father. I went out to the barn and—"

Buck let out a soft chuckle. "Oh, so that's what you two were talking about. Well, in that case, Cody's right. I do know everything. I'll bet you climbed up into the hayloft and fell asleep, just like when you were a little girl."

He directed his comments toward Cody. "She was always doing that. Whenever it was her nap time she would sneak off and we'd find her sleeping up in the hayloft. The first time she disappeared like that her mother and I were frantic. We searched everywhere and were about to call the sheriff when Tom Collier found her up there." He turned toward Melanie again. "You really gave us a scare, honey."

Melanie had to look away. The warmth in her father's eyes made her uncomfortable. That was not the way she had remembered it at all. She had always thought that her father had been too busy even to notice that she was not in her room and that he had made her mother continue working rather than go in search of her. She never realized that they both knew exactly where she had been and that she was safe.

Buck's appetite actually seemed a little better. He had not been able to eat any lunch for the past two weeks and had only picked at his breakfast and dinner. Cody was pleased that not only had he eaten breakfast, he had actually eaten a bit of lunch, too. Cody toyed with the thought that perhaps his concerns about Melanie upsetting Buck had been unfounded. He also toyed with the thought that maybe he was more than casually interested in Buck Winslow's wayward daughter for reasons far more personal than merely seeing that Buck was happy.

"Cody, why don't you take Mel on that tour now? While you're doing that I'll go into the office and finish up on the computer."

Melanie noticed the expression that darted across Cody's face, but it was gone before she could identify it. She could not tell if it related to his showing her around or her father's comment about doing work with the computer, but either way it did not leave her with a positive feeling. Buck seemed to be oblivious to Cody's brief flash of irritation as he continued with his conversation.

"I'm sorry I haven't been able to spend very much time with you this morning, honey. But, then—" a broad smile covered Buck's face; his eyes sparkled with good humor and his tone of voice teased her "—it seems you spent the morning snoozing in the hayloft.'' He reached out and gave her hand a loving squeeze. "The three of us can sit down and have a nice family get-together this evening after we have dinner.''

Family get-together? Had she heard her father correctly? The *three* of them a family? Melanie shot an incensed glare at Cody. That was something the *two* of them would definitely discuss as soon as they were away from her father. In spite of her most carefully guarded inner thoughts and hopes, it appeared that her suspicions about Cody were turning out to be correct after all. He was taking advantage of her father's diminished capabilities for his own personal gain. She wondered what tidbit of information would be revealed next. What she did not understand was the stab of dismay she felt at being right rather than the outrage at Cody for what he was doing. Somewhere deep inside she had hoped she was wrong—perhaps as much for her sake as for her father's.

As if being able to read her mind, Buck addressed Melanie's thoughts. "I'm so glad to see you and Cody getting along so well. He's like family, you know. He's been just like a son to me. I don't know what I would have done without his help and friendship.''

Cody saw Melanie stiffen but was not sure exactly what had caused it. He was beginning to relax around her a bit and she seemed to be holding to their tenuous agreement to not display any signs of disharmony around Buck. He had been truly surprised by her response—what appeared to him to be genuine sorrow—to the news of her father's imminent demise. He thought he had her pegged, but now he wasn't so sure. Perhaps he had been too hasty in his judgment. He hoped so.

"We'll see you a little later, Buck.'' Cody placed his hand in the middle of Melanie's back as she rose from the kitchen chair, and guided her across the room. He paused for a moment when they reached the door, calling back over his shoulder. "Don't overdo it. I'll give you a hand with the computer stuff when I get back."

As soon as they left the kitchen Melanie whirled around toward Cody. Her eyes narrowed and the angry golden flecks ignited. "What is all of this *like a son* stuff?"

He bristled at her rapid mood change, speaking through clenched teeth as his fingers tightened around her arm. "Not here." He hurried toward the front door, practically dragging her behind him. He did not slow his fast pace until they were across the yard and inside the barn.

As soon as he stopped walking she wrenched her arm free of his grasp. "I told you not to manhandle me." She glared at him, her words as hostile as her eyes. "Don't you ever grab me like that again."

"And I told you not to say anything in front of Buck that would cause him even a moment's concern." He leaned in toward her, the sharp set of his jaw making his expression seem even more formidable than he had intended. The intensity of the moment caused her to blink a couple of times and physically step back in retreat from the almost overpowering strength of his stare. "Consider yourself warned for the last time. I will do whatever I need to do to make sure his final days are comfortable and pleasant, and that includes locking you inside this barn if that's what it takes."

Mel could not believe her ears. She lashed out in anger at this overbearing interloper. "How dare you threaten me!"

As mad as she was with him she could not deny the magnetic pull that reached out and grabbed hold of her senses. Too many things were happening all at once, too many totally unexpected things. She felt a twinge of guilt over her errant thoughts. She had returned to the ranch to attempt some sort of an understanding with her father, not to in-

dulge silly schoolgirl palpitations over this big, blond hunk
of a cowboy who made her insides quiver and had her common sense twisted in a knot of confusion. The last thing that
should have been on her mind was any type of personal interest in this arrogant, bossy and incredibly sexy man.

Cody stood his ground, not giving her an inch of room to
maneuver. "I'm not threatening you. I'm simply telling you
the way it is and the way it's going to be."

The air bristled with the energy that surged between them.
Melanie was determined to hold her position against him,
not back down from his aggressive stance. She had handled
many magazine assignments that had required a tricky
combination of both tenacity and a cool, logical head. She
had plenty of tenacity, but for some reason she did not seem
to be able to maintain that cool head, or a cool anything
else, around Cody Chandler. Everything about him equated
with heat—heated anger and heated desires.

Melanie shoved aside her yearnings in an effort to get
back to the matter at hand. She forced a hardness to her
words, an edge she was finding more difficult to maintain
through each ensuing confrontation with Cody. "I want to
know what this *like a son* business is all about. Just what are
you trying to pull here? Is this some sort of scam? Preying
on the emotions of a dying man?"

It was not what she meant to say, not what she intended
to imply. The words had sprung from her mouth before she
could stop them. She saw the look on his face, the way he
recoiled in shock as if he had been physically attacked.

He clenched his jaw, took in a deep breath and slowly let
it out. He narrowed his eyes and stretched himself to his full
height, making every effort to tower over her as much as
possible. She could not have hit him in a more vulnerable
spot if she had tried. He knew her angry, irrational accusations should not have had any effect on him. But, then, why

had they caused that quick jab of emotional pain? He tried to drive the hurt away. He measured every word, his voice harsh and cold. "There's only one person in this barn who is responsible for any wrongdoing or has inflicted any harm on Buck, and it's not me."

Any guilt or regret she might have felt over her rash statement immediately disappeared, igniting a volatile exchange of words. "How dare you—"

"Don't try to hand me that indignant act. If Buck thinks of me as a son, then maybe it's because you were never—"

"Maybe he wanted a son but what he got was a daughter!" She could not hold back the tears as a lifetime of hurt overflowed the place inside where she had tried to lock it away. "A daughter he ignored and never really wanted." A sob caught in her throat and the rest of her words came out in a hushed quaver. "A daughter who would have given anything if only her father had loved her."

Four

If Melanie's earlier allegations about his honesty shocked Cody, then her tears really threw him for a loop. There was no doubt in his mind that Buck Winslow adored his daughter and had been through his own private hell. Buck had suffered the untimely loss of his wife only to have the emotional upheaval compounded when his only child had taken off for parts unknown.

Cody felt at a total loss. He did not know whether to be angry at Melanie for her personal attack against him, take her to task for her erroneous comments about Buck or attempt to comfort the obviously distraught woman, who was going through her own emotional stress. Her pain showed through the sheen of tears that filled her eyes. The tender feelings he had been trying to suppress from the moment he turned on the living-room light and saw her sprawled on the floor finally won out.

He was not sure what to say to her, but he did know what to do. He reached out and gently wiped away the wet trails that ran down her cheeks, then he pulled her into his arms and wrapped her in the warmth of his embrace. He threaded his fingers through her hair and nestled her head against his shoulder.

An almost inaudible sigh escaped his throat as he took a calming breath. His words came out in a whisper. "Tell me, Melanie Winslow, why are you here? Why did you pick this time to show up? You said you didn't know about Buck's health—"

The warm feeling he had coaxed through the thin shield of Mel's hostility did not last long. She snapped her head back and started to shove away from him. "Do you think I—"

He placed his fingertips against her lips to silence what had started as yet another angry outburst. "It seems our agreed upon truce didn't last very long the first time. What do you say to giving it another try? I believe what you said about not being aware of Buck's health. I'm just trying to get straight in my mind exactly why you're here." He lifted her chin with his fingertips until he could look fully into her face and eyes. "What is it you want?" He felt the length of her body press against his as she tentatively returned his embrace. His voice took on a husky quality. "Why did you come back?"

"I . . . I'm not sure." She could barely get out the words. The full force of his magnetism had totally and completely enveloped her. It was hard to tell which of them made the first move, whether he lowered his head or she raised hers, but a moment later his lips were on hers. The same quiver of excitement passed through her body as had earlier that day when she awoke in the hayloft to find he was real, not just part of her dream. His mouth insisted without being demanding. His kiss crystallized one thought beyond any doubt—she wanted more of him, so very much more.

He had not been sure about kissing her, had not made it a conscious part of his conduct. It had almost been an involuntary action, much like breathing. But now that he had started he did not want to stop. Her mouth was soft and sensual, her taste every bit as delicious as he knew it would be. He flicked his tongue across her lower lip, fully intending to explore what lay beyond.

"Hey, Cody! Are you in there?"

The shout had come from the side door of the barn, completely shattering the tender moment they were sharing—a moment that was on the verge of bursting into flame.

Ross Andrews shuffled through the door, squinting as his eyes adjusted to the dim light. A sense of urgency surrounded him as he peered around inside the barn. "Cody, is that—"

"Damn!" Cody whispered the word against Melanie's lips. She quickly tried to pull back from him. She could almost feel the crimson flush of embarrassment spread across her cheeks.

"Oops!" Ross came to an abrupt halt when he saw that Cody was not alone. "Uh, sorry to interrupt, but I thought you'd want to know..." He glanced down at the ground, obviously flustered by the scene he had accidentally stumbled upon.

Cody placed his fingertips against Melanie's lips. His words were soft and held a world of promise. "We will continue this discussion about our little difference of opinion at a later time." He placed a quick kiss on the tip of her nose, released her from his embrace, then turned toward Ross.

"Thought I'd want to know about what?" Cody fixed him with an inquiring gaze. "Is there some kind of a problem, Ross?"

Ross Andrews glanced questioningly at Melanie, then back at Cody. He shifted his weight from one foot to the other, displaying his discomfort over the awkward situation.

"Ross, this is Melanie Winslow...Buck's daughter." He noted the surprise on Ross's face at this bit of information. Ross had been employed at the ranch almost as long as Cody and had heard about Buck's absent daughter.

"Melanie, this is Ross Andrews. He's head wrangler and assistant foreman. I've had to rely heavily on him the past few months, what with Buck's..."

Cody's voice trailed off. Everyone knew what it was he had started to say.

Melanie held out her hand. "It's a pleasure to meet you, Ross."

Ross quickly pulled off his leather work glove to accept her handshake. "Pleasure's mine, ma'am. Me and the boys was wonderin' who owned the car with the California license plates."

So many new faces she had never seen before, and not just ranch hands, either. There were new people with responsible positions. Melanie noted the curiosity on Ross's face and in his eyes. She wondered what he was thinking, what he had heard about her, what opinions he had formed.

It had never occurred to her that there would be so many people at the ranch whom she had never met. She had assumed that things would be as she had left them. Only things were not the same—nothing was the same.

"I think the world of your daddy, Miss Winslow." Ross politely tipped the brim of his hat, pulled on his glove and returned his attention to Cody. "It's Moonglow. According to the calendar she ain't due to drop her foal for five days, but she's givin' off signs that say she could drop early."

Cody knitted his brow in concentration. "Hmm...this is her first foal. You'd better alert the vet. Does it look like she's going to have problems?"

"No, not really. Just the typical signs that she's getting ready to drop. She's doing a lot of pacing in her stall, keeps turnin' her head to look back along her flanks and nips at her sides. Her udder doesn't show any gray waxing yet. We're keepin' an eye on 'er."

"Let's go see." Cody started toward the barn door. He was all business, giving no hint to indicate that anything untoward might have been going on prior to Ross's arrival.

But Cody's kiss still burned hot on Melanie's lips and in her mind. She tried to regain her senses and composure. She felt the same weakness in her knees as when he had picked her up and carried her into the hallway outside his bedroom door. She watched as Cody and Ross left the barn, only vaguely aware of what they had said to each other.

The only words still in her head were the ones Cody had spoken to her about their *little difference of opinion*. It seemed to her that they had been engaged in much more than a little difference of opinion. It was more like a full-fledged battle. How had things suddenly gone from a heated argument to a heated kiss that had burned right down to her toes?

She was not sure what to think. If his plan had been to confuse the issue and divert attention from her suspicions, then he had nearly succeeded ...*if* that had been his intention. In spite of the accusations she had made to his face, she was beginning to wonder if he really was the devious person she originally believed him to be. She also wondered if it was her logic talking or her desires. Exactly what was in charge, her head or her libido?

Melanie left the barn, pausing to look down the drive toward the stables. She spotted Cody in conversation with Ross. She turned and walked slowly toward the house. Perhaps now would be a good opportunity for her to spend some time alone with her father. That was the reason for her return to the ranch, and according to what Cody had told her, she had better hurry or her trip would be in vain.

A crash reached Melanie's ears as she opened the front door. The sound was immediately followed by Edna's voice.

"Buck? Are you all right?"

There was only silence in response to Edna's call. A shiver of trepidation darted through Melanie's body. She hurried inside. Buck was not in the living room. She met Edna rushing in from the kitchen. They exchanged a quick look of concern as Edna turned toward the office with Mel right behind her.

Melanie came to an abrupt halt when she spotted her father lying on the floor, an overturned end table next to him. Pieces of a broken lamp were scattered around the table. A faint moan escaped his lips, but he did not move. She rushed to him. The panic welled into her throat and her mouth went dry. He looked so pale and weak.

Melanie knelt beside him, taking his limp hand in hers. As before, his skin was icy cold. Her voice was a hushed whisper as she fought back the sob of fear. "Father?" She rubbed his hand, trying to bring some warmth to it. "Say something, Father. Are you all right?"

Edna's response to the emergency was immediate and efficient. "You keep talking to him, try to get his mind focused on your voice. I'll get Cody and phone for the doctor."

She heard Edna go out the front door, heard the urgency in her voice as she shouted for Cody to come quickly. Melanie looked at her father lying on the floor, so helpless and so lifeless. Tears filled her eyes. She blinked them away. "Father? Talk to me. Say something. This isn't fair. It can't end like this."

Her words grew more emphatic as some of her pent-up anger made its way to the surface. "I was never able to do anything to please you. I was never allowed to be part of your life back then—" a sob caught in her throat "—but I'll be damned if I'll let you shut me out now!" The tears trickled down her cheeks; her voice became a frightened whisper. "All I ever wanted was for you to notice me, to give me just one little word of praise or encouragement." She tried to gulp in a calming breath of air. Her voice quavered with emotion. "Talk to me, Father. Say something. You can't leave me now, not yet . . . not like this."

Cody paused at the door in reaction to Melanie's plaintive words. He heard her pain and inner turmoil. He was also beginning to gain some insight into why she had decided to return to the ranch. Perhaps she was not as much of an enigma as he had first thought. He quickly shoved the thoughts aside. Buck needed help. This was certainly not the first time he had fallen, but it could be the last.

Cody stepped in and took charge of things. "Edna, get a couple of blankets." He bent down next to Melanie. "I don't want to move him. I don't know where he hit or how he fell. We can't take a chance on a neck or back injury. We'll cover him and keep him warm. Doc Gerrard was on his way here for his regular visit. He's only about fifteen minutes away." He turned toward Melanie, his calm manner projecting control and eliciting confidence. "Why don't you pick up these broken lamp pieces so no one else gets injured?"

"Here you are, Cody." Edna handed him one of the blankets, then she unfolded the other one. They quickly covered Buck, tucking in the blankets along his body.

Melanie picked up the larger pieces and threw them in the wastebasket, then swept up the smaller pieces. Her insides had not stopped quivering from the moment she saw her father lying on the office floor. She was thankful that Cody had taken control the way he had. Even though she was normally levelheaded, she was not sure she could have maintained the type of calm he brought to the situation.

She sank to her knees next to Cody. "Is he—"

Buck's eyelids fluttered, then his eyes slowly opened. He looked around. He seemed dazed, but he was conscious. His gaze lit on Cody for a moment, then settled on Melanie. He tried to reach out from under the blanket as he attempted a weak smile.

"You just stay still, Father. The doctor should be here any minute." She tucked the blanket back in along his shoulder. She tried to sound as calm and in control as Cody. "You gave us quite a scare."

Buck's voice faltered, as if the mere effort of speaking was too taxing. "I'm not sure what happened, honey. I must have tripped over something. I guess I just wasn't watching where I was going. That's certainly not like me."

Melanie glanced at Cody, who shook his head, indicating that things were not the way Buck was trying to make them seem.

"He should sleep for the rest of the night." Dr. Gerrard closed his medical bag and walked out to the front porch, accompanied by Cody. He had stayed for dinner, as he always did on his weekly visits. "It was truly a miracle that he didn't break any bones. But, then, the fact that he's been able to get around at all for the past month, let alone on his own, is in itself miraculous. I swear, Cody, I really don't know what's kept him going. He's a true testimonial to what sheer willpower can accomplish."

Cody glanced through the window at Melanie, who was helping Edna with the dishes. Could she be the reason? He reluctantly pulled his attention away from his thoughts about Melanie and returned it to what the doctor was saying.

"...hospital bed sent out first thing in the morning. Even if he thinks he can get up, I don't want him trying it. He simply doesn't have the strength. Unless Buck has some objections, I think the bed could be set up right where his bed is now. The parlor is large and sunny and he has a good view out the corner windows, so he'll be able to watch what's going on. It won't be the same as being there, but it will at least give him a partial sense of participation."

"I'll see to it that he stays down." Cody stared at the ground, then off to the horizon for a moment. "Tell me, Doc, what are we looking at? I know he's been kind of skirting around the edges of borrowed time, but just how much time does he have?"

Dr. Gerrard took in a deep breath, then slowly let it out. He glanced through the window at Melanie, then stepped off the porch and made his way toward his car, Cody walking with him. "To tell you truthfully, I don't really see much reason to even send out the hospital bed. I'd say he only has a few days left."

Cody, too, drew a deep breath and slowly let it out. "I see."

"Does his daughter know how serious he is? I was surprised to see her here. Buck never mentioned that he was expecting her."

"He wasn't. She showed up about four-thirty this morning." Cody paced a couple of steps back and forth, then came to an abrupt halt and faced the doctor, the annoyance bristling inside him. "I didn't even know who she was, for God's sake. I thought it was someone trying to break into the house." The memory of his body pinning hers to the floor was now even more unsettling to him in light of the delicious kiss they had shared not long ago—a kiss that had promised a whole lot more.

"I'm also sending a nurse along with the hospital bed. I want someone with him around the clock. You have my cellular phone number and my beeper. Be sure to call me if there's any change."

It had been a long and emotionally exhausting day. Cody watched the doctor drive away, then went back to the house. He needed to check on the entries Buck had made in the computer and execute the necessary corrections. It created a double work load for him, having to redo everything Buck had done, but there was no way Cody could deny his friend that one last vestige of feeling that he was still making a contribution to the running of the ranch. He paused at the door of the parlor.

Melanie sat in a chair by the bed, watching Buck as he slept. The doctor had not told her much, but it was obvious things were very bad. She did not know what to do. She felt a hand come down on her shoulder and looked up to see Cody standing next to her. She placed her hand on top of his. It was an involuntary gesture on her part, a response to the comfort she felt just knowing he was there.

"The doctor says Buck should sleep all the way through the night. Come on, there's nothing you can do sitting here."

"What... what else did the doctor say?"

Cody coaxed her out of the chair and escorted her to the door. "He said he was sending a nurse first thing in the morning. He wants Buck to have around-the-clock care from now on."

"From now on?" A shiver went through Melanie's body as the full implication of Cody's words hit her. She searched his face for any indication of the truth. She tried her best to hold back the sob. "This is the end, isn't it?"

He studied the apprehension that covered her features. It touched him at an emotional depth greater than he wanted to admit. "Come on, let's take a walk."

Melanie looked back at her father, then allowed Cody to lead her out of the house.

Cody could see she was deep in thought. It seemed to him that it would be an intrusion to interrupt it. They walked along in silence. He guided her toward the stables. He wanted to check with Ross on any changes with Moonglow.

Buck had been concerned about Moonglow's foal. Perhaps breeding the mare for the first time, and now the imminent arrival of that new life, coincided with coming to terms with his own mortality.

They stopped at Moonglow's stall. Ross was inside with the mare. "Any changes in her condition?"

Ross turned around at the sound of Cody's voice. As he had before, he glanced questioningly at Melanie.

She turned toward Cody. "I'll just look around while the two of you discuss your business."

Melanie stood outside the stables. Even though Cody had not shown her what was new and different, as her father had requested, she could see many of the improvements. The obvious ones were cosmetic in nature—new fences, painted a gleaming white, had been erected along the drive and around the house, and what used to be the gravel road in from the highway had been paved. Three rugged four-wheel-drive vehicles and a one-ton pickup truck with a shell were parked in a new carport along with the horse trailers, all painted to match and displaying the ranch's brand on the doors.

She wandered toward the small building attached to the carport. The door was locked. She peered through the window. It looked like a small communications office. She spotted five cellular phones, eight walkie-talkies plugged into chargers, and a base station. She was sure she would find the same type of up-to-date equipment everywhere.

"Well, what do you think?"

Melanie whirled around at the sound of Cody's voice. "My father was right. Things certainly have changed around here. The entire ranch seems to be a model of state-of-the-art efficiency."

A sudden idea hit her. She had not come to the ranch for any reason other than the personal one of attempting a reconciliation with her father, but as she looked around she began visualizing a magazine article, complete with photo layout, on the workings of a modern cattle ranch—a marriage of yesterday's cowboy and today's technology. She allowed the idea to turn over in her mind, to take shape and develop substance.

The last fading streaks of sunset splashed golden across Cody's face, accentuating his ruggedly handsome features. His weathered hat was tilted at just the right angle and his leather work gloves were tucked under his belt. He looked every bit the cowboy, yet apparently felt equally at home in front of a computer. He epitomized what the article would depict.

"It's almost dark." Cody's intrusion into her thoughts startled her. "I suggest we postpone that tour until tomorrow morning. Besides—" she felt his hand against her back and a gentle pressure as he guided her toward the main drive "—I'm sure you must be exhausted by now."

"Yes. To tell you truthfully, I am tired. I think a good night's sleep is exactly what I need."

They returned to the house. Cody paused outside her bedroom and leaned against the doorjamb. "I promise you that tour first thing in the morning." He reached out and tucked an errant strand of hair behind her ear, then allowed his fingertip to trail across her cheek before dropping his hand to his side.

Melanie Winslow had gotten under his skin. It was not the same thing as a splinter that created an irritation. Quite the contrary. It was a warm sensation that made him want more.

Melanie felt every degree of the heat generated by Cody's nearness. She still had not classified Cody Chandler, but she did know exactly how he made her feel—and she was not happy about it. He somehow had managed to totally capture her in his spell.

"Well, uh, I think I'd better take care of a few things. I never did have an opportunity to unpack this morning." She ran her fingers through her hair in an effort to stop the nervous tension that flitted through her body.

"I guess I'll see you tomorrow then." He could not take his eyes off her, nor could he quell the desire to take up exactly where they had left off in the barn. He leaned his face into hers, paused for the briefest of moments, then seized her all-too-tempting mouth full on. He wrapped her in his arms and pulled her body tight against his. He felt her warmth radiate to him as surely as if he had been standing next to a cozy fireplace.

The heat that had been sizzling between them burst into flame. Melanie was once again drawn into the magnetic pull of his masculinity. His kiss excited her in a way she had not experienced in many years. She slipped her arms around his neck and responded with a fervor that matched his. This cowboy was not her type of man, the ranch was not her life-

style. It was her last negative thought. She had never before been kissed with the level of intensity and passion that
emanated from Cody Chandler.

Her willpower and ability to resist his advances drained
away. She knew this had to stop before it went too far. She
mustered all the resistance she could and finally broke off
the kiss. "I . . . I need to unpack." Her body was alive with
the sensations of his touch, the way one arm still held her
tightly against his hard torso as he cupped her chin in his
free hand. He was as addictive as any narcotic and every bit
as dangerous. She was not sure exactly where any of this
would lead, but she instinctively knew there could be no
such thing as a casual flirtation with this man. He was too
intense in his passions. It would be all or nothing.

Cody saw the golden flecks in her eyes, but they did not
shoot sparks of anger. This time they were burning embers
of desire, a beckoning that threatened to pull him in much
farther than he wanted or could control. "I have work to do,
too." He traced the outline of her upper lip as he took a
calming breath. "I'll see you in the morning."

Melanie retreated into her room, closing the door behind
her. She heard Cody walk down the hall. Leaning back
against the door, she closed her eyes. Her heart pounded in
her chest. He was dangerous to be around, emotionally
dangerous. She set her jaw in a line of determination. There
would be no more of this kissing stuff. She would keep her
distance. She still did not know what he was all about. She
fully intended to phone her father's attorney in the morning. She picked up one of her suitcases, placed it in the
middle of the bed and opened it.

Cody went to the office. Now that Buck was asleep for the
night he had lots of work to do, lots of changes to make in
the accounts. He certainly had not anticipated the type of

interference caused by the unexpected arrival of Melanie Winslow.

He sat for a moment, his thoughts returning to his most recent encounter with her. She might have the same delicately beautiful features as her mother, but there was no doubt she was Buck Winslow's daughter. She was independent, stubborn, strong-willed and determined. His inner stress softened and he relaxed his tensed muscles. She was also far too tempting. Nothing lasting could ever develop between them. She wanted the big city, the bright lights and the fast lane. He had already been there and did not want to go back.

He flipped on the computer and watched as it went through its start-up process. He busied himself making changes to most of what Buck had done earlier that day. He also needed to make a phone call.

In her room, Melanie finished her unpacking, then grabbed a pad of paper and sat at the desk, the same one she sat at to do her homework when she was in high school. The article about modern cattle ranching had solidified in her mind and she wanted to get her thoughts down on paper before she forgot them. As soon as she had a loose outline together she would call Jeff, her agent, and pitch the idea to him.

There was more to her desire to work on the article than just the fact that she thought it was a marketable idea. She wanted to keep her mind busy. Nothing was as she'd expected it to be when she turned off the highway and drove up the road to the ranch. Even though she had not yet formulated the thought into actual words, she had made the decision to stay at the ranch for the remainder of the time her father had left.

She had not given any thought to what would happen when her father passed away. Wills, inheritance, probate...none of it had occurred to her. She did not even know the extent of her father's estate. Beyond the ranch, she had no idea what he owned. She did not even know the financial status of the ranch, other than it looked very successful and her father had said it was prosperous.

And then there was Cody Chandler. He was the other reason she needed to provide herself with something to occupy her mind. She did not know what else to do about her attraction to him. She closed her eyes for a moment in an attempt to force his image from her mind...and possibly from her heart. She opened her eyes. Work. She needed to get to work. The ideas were fresh in her mind, the images alive. She started on her outline.

In the other part of the house, Cody leaned back in his chair and stared at the computer monitor. He had made all the changes to what Buck had done and then designated several payments to be made the next day. Finally, he arranged a transfer of cash from one account to another. Now he had a phone call to make, then he could retire to his room and do some reading before going to bed...assuming he could get his thoughts off Melanie Winslow, a mighty iffy assumption at best. He reached for the phone.

Mel went over her notes again, making some changes as she read through them. She was satisfied with what she had come up with. In fact, she was excited about the way the piece was coming together. It had all the makings of a great magazine layout. She toyed with the idea of waiting until morning to call Jeff but changed her mind. As soon as she lifted the receiver she realized someone else was using the phone. She started to hang up, when something she heard caught her attention. She recognized Cody's voice.

"...changed Buck's entries in the cash account and reallocated most of the expenses. I set up those payments we discussed. They'll be done tomorrow. We're about out of time. If we can't get that two hundred thousand transferred it could end up as part of the estate.''

Melanie carefully replaced the receiver in the cradle. What she heard had upset her . . . and confused her.

Five

Melanie was awake early the next morning. She had spent a very restless night in spite of the fact that she had gotten an adequate amount of sleep. She could not get the snippet of conversation out of her mind. She did not know what Cody Chandler was up to, but she knew he was doing something behind her father's back—something to do with the ranch's accounts and her father's money to the tune of two hundred thousand dollars. She would call Henry Sanderson, her father's attorney, as soon as his office opened.

She checked her camera equipment, loaded film and cleaned filters and lenses. Then she slung her favorite camera over her shoulder, grabbed the camera bag and headed toward the kitchen. By the time she had some coffee it would be sunrise, her favorite time of day. She wanted shots showing a working cattle ranch starting its morning, then she would spend some time looking over the improvements and planning her shots for the next day. Jeff had been very

enthusiastic when she had finally talked to him. He said he
wanted to see the completed article as soon as possible.

She paused by the door to the parlor. Her father seemed
to be sleeping. She quietly entered the room and crossed to
his bedside. Several prescription bottles rested on the
nightstand. She picked up one of the bottles and looked at
the label. She recognized it as a very strong painkiller.

Her stomach twisted into a hard knot. Even though her
father's illness had taken an obvious physical toll on him,
even though Cody had told her that there was not much time
left and the doctor's visit had confirmed this, she still had
not fully comprehended the severity of it all. It had not occurred to her that he would be in the amount of pain that
would require that particular medication. As she stared at
what used to be a forceful and commanding presence, the
full realization finally sank in. The tears filled her eyes and
trickled down her cheeks.

She set her camera and gadget bag on the floor, pulled a
chair over next to the bed and sat down. Would it end like
this? According to a couple of books she had read it was
possible to come to terms with differences even after the
parent in question had died, but she did not want it to be
that way. As she watched her father sleep she realized just
how much she wanted everything to be okay.

"Here you are, sweetie." Edna thrust a mug of steaming
coffee in front of Mel. "I just made it."

She had not heard Edna enter the room, but was grateful
to see the coffee. She accepted the mug. "Thanks. It smells
good." She took a sip, then offered Edna an appreciative
smile.

Edna lingered by the bed. She shuffled her weight from
one foot to the other in a nervous manner, then finally said
what was on her mind. "Buck has told me all about you,
many times over. He's really proud of you. He's followed

your career very closely. I know he told you that yesterday. He really meant it, you know." She paused, as if trying to gather her thoughts. "I'm happy you decided to come back . . . while there was still time."

Melanie could see the sadness in Edna's eyes, and something else. There was also genuine affection there. She suddenly felt very uncomfortable and out of place. Cody had as much as threatened her if she upset Buck. Edna obviously cared very much for Buck. Ross Andrews had reacted oddly when Cody had introduced them. She had noticed furtive sidelong glances from a couple of the ranch hands she had seen by the stables. She had grown up here, spent the first eighteen years of her life on the ranch, yet she felt like a stranger. An outsider intruding into their daily lives.

She took another sip of her coffee. Her words were whispered. She could not hide her emotional stress. "I had no idea he was ill, let alone at death's—" She could not finish her sentence.

"I know Buck's real pleased that you've come home. It's almost all he talked about yesterday morning after you left the kitchen." Edna paused for a moment, then continued. "I know it's not my place to say, but I think hoping he'd see you again is what kept him going the past month or so. I don't know what kind of miracle it was that brought you here at this time, but I thank the good Lord for it."

Edna glanced down at the floor, then looked at Melanie again. "Well, I need to get back to my work." She reached out and gave Mel's hand a little squeeze, then quickly left the parlor.

Mel sat in silence, sipping her coffee and staring out the window. The first gray streaks of dawn were visible. She glanced at her father, who appeared to still be asleep. She gathered her camera equipment and left the parlor. She did not want to wake her father from his much-needed rest.

The sunrise painted the morning sky with the bright colors of a new day. The distant horizon held a scattering of clouds, a portent of the forecast rainstorm. Melanie chose her shots, capturing the early-morning chores while making sure that she stayed out of everyone's way. She spent a busy three hours reacquainting herself with the daily routine of a working ranch. Even though she was not consciously looking for Cody, she was aware of his absence from the scene.

She returned her equipment to her bedroom, then hurried to the parlor. Right now her prime objective was to be at her father's side when he woke. She was not sure how to say what she wanted to, or even sure what it was that she wanted to say, but she had to try while there was still time. She stopped by the kitchen and poured herself another cup of coffee, taking it with her. She settled into the chair next to her father's bed, placing the mug on the table next to her. She leaned back and closed her eyes.

The sound of Buck's voice finally penetrated into Melanie's consciousness. She jerked upright and shook the sleep from her head. She had not intended to fall asleep. She was sure she had only dozed off for a moment. She opened her eyes and saw Buck trying to sit up. She jumped up from the chair and was immediately at his side.

"Father...don't try to get up. You're supposed to stay in bed." She smoothed his blanket and tucked it in along the sides of the bed. "Can I get something for you?"

He extended a weak smile and reached out a shaky hand toward her. "Melanie, honey, just having you home is all I ever wanted."

His words were said with such honesty, such openness. Her eyes filled with tears. His touch was every bit as cold as it had been the day before, but this time she did not pull her hand away. She returned his squeeze and smiled as best she could.

She tried to sound casual and upbeat as she attempted light conversation. "I've been shooting some photographs this morning. I thought I might do an article about modern cattle ranching. My agent really likes the idea."

"That's nice, honey. You might want to check with Cody first, make sure it's okay with him." Buck's manner was distracted, as if he had something else on his mind and was only half listening to what she had said.

She forced a calm to her voice, not wanting her irritation to show. "Why should I need to clear a magazine article with Cody? It's your ranch, not his."

"Now, Melanie. I want you and Cody to get along. He's very important to our operation here and in the days ahead . . . well, I know I don't have much time left—"

"Now, don't talk like that, Father." She was still fighting to keep her voice calm and level, only this time she was not doing battle with irritation. She desperately wanted to keep the tremor out of it.

"Don't try to pacify me, Mel. One thing about this disease . . . it sure turns the volume knob up real good on the hearing." He looked up at her, his eyes filled with the insight of a man who had made peace with himself and was prepared for what he knew would soon be. "I can hear people standing on the front porch talking. I can hear what's going on, even when everyone thinks I'm sleeping." He tried to chuckle, but it dissolved into a coughing spasm. "I can even hear Edna in the kitchen slicing bread."

"Maybe you shouldn't try to talk right now. Can I get you something? Some coffee, or maybe something to eat?" Thousands of emotions crashed around inside her, colliding into one another and bouncing off her consciousness.

She did not know what she was feeling, did not know what to think.

"Yes, you can get something for me. In my bedroom—" he paused to catch his breath "—in my bedroom, on the shelf in the closet, is a cardboard carton with a piece of cord tied around it. Could you get it for me?"

"Sure, Father." He seemed so weak. It was obvious that even the minimal effort required to talk was taxing for him. "I'll be right back."

Buck sank into the bed and closed his eyes. His breathing was shallow but steady. Melanie watched him for a moment longer, then left the parlor and went to his bedroom.

She found the box, coaxing it off the shelf with her fingertips and catching it as it fell. It was heavy and dusty. It appeared to have been tucked away in the closet for a long time. She wondered what was in it that was so important to her father. She wiped off the outside of the carton, then carried it back to his bedside.

Buck opened his eyes when she came into the room. His gaze immediately lit on the box she carried. "Yes, that's the one. Bring it over here, Mel, honey. Open it up."

She set the box on the edge of his bed and slipped the cord off from around it. A nervousness jittered inside her stomach. She had no idea what was in the box, but for some reason the prospect of finding out filled her with apprehension. She glanced up at her father. She could see it in his face, see how anxious he was for her to open the box. She lifted the lid. Her fingers trembled in spite of her best efforts to prevent it.

The box was filled with notebooks and journals. She recognized her mother's handwriting on the covers of several of the books. She felt a hard lump settle in her chest. It refused to rise to her throat and would not sink to her stomach. It seemed to be pushing against her chest, making it difficult for her to breathe.

"Those are for you, Mel. They're Virginia's writings. Your mother began writing in those books the day we were married. She wrote in them every single day, right up until the day—" Buck was unable to finish his sentence. He laid his head back on his pillow and closed his eyes. His chest heaved several times as a couple of sobs caught in his throat. His face contorted in a painful expression.

"Father! What's wrong?" Melanie felt the panic rising inside her. "Do you need something?" She turned toward the door. "Edna! Come quickly!"

Melanie had to strain to hear Buck's words. "No, I don't need anything. I'm fine. Don't disturb Edna."

Edna rushed into the parlor, wiping her hands on her apron. "What's wrong?"

"It's Father—I'm not sure..."

Melanie watched as Edna took charge.

Edna removed two tablets from one of the prescription bottles and one tablet from another. Without a wasted minute she gave Buck his medication. Melanie felt so useless, so totally helpless. "Edna, I...I'm sorry to bother you. It's just that I didn't know what to do."

"Don't you worry about it, sweetie. I've been taking care of Buck for so long now that it's just second nature for me." She glanced toward her employer. He had calmed down and seemed to be resting more comfortably. "The pain wouldn't hit him like that if he took his pills when he was supposed to. Buck is really a stubborn mule when it comes to his medication. He just won't take it at his regularly scheduled times unless someone makes him do it."

Edna glanced at the cardboard carton Melanie had opened, then looked at Melanie. "Well, I see Buck finally allowed someone to open that box. I've worked for him going on ten years and he never let me touch it. Guess he's been saving it for you.''

Edna checked on Buck again, then returned to her chores. Melanie plopped into the chair and sat without moving. She felt drained, almost limp from exhaustion, even though she had not actually done anything.

She returned her attention to the box filled with Virginia Winslow's journals. She stared at them without touching them. In eighteen years she had never seen her mother write in a journal. She never knew they existed. Her father had saved them all these years, saved them so he could give them to her. Feelings about her father that had once been so clearly defined in her mind were becoming obscure and shadowed.

She tentatively reached out and picked up the top notebook. She ran her fingertips lightly across the cover, pausing as she read the label. It contained a Roman numeral one and underneath that was the date of her mother and father's wedding. She took a deep breath, then slowly let it out as she opened the book.

''Edna, are you here?'' Cody called from the hallway.

Melanie quickly closed the journal and replaced it in the box. The journals contained her mother's private words and thoughts. They certainly were not any one else's business. She turned just in time to meet Cody at the door of the parlor.

''I believe Edna's in the kitchen.''

His attitude changed from harried to mischievous in response to finding Melanie in the parlor. ''Well, good morning. I trust you got a good night's sleep.'' He purposely looked her up and down, then allowed his gaze to linger on her face. His line of sight dropped to her mouth and remained there—that very tempting mouth that tasted sweeter than anything he could remember.

"Yes, I slept just fine. Thank you." Cody Chandler made her blood rush hot and fast. There was just no other way to say it. The memory of his kiss made her hungry for more.

"I saw you out taking some snapshots this morning."

"Snapshots?" The word grated against her sensibilities. "I'm a professional photojournalist. I don't take *snapshots*."

"Melanie tells me she wants to do a magazine article about us, something about modern cattle ranching." Buck turned his head to look at Cody. "What do you think about that?"

"Well..." Cody studied her for a moment. He saw it in her eyes, those golden flecks revving up for yet another clash of wills between them. Perhaps at some other time he might have welcomed the opportunity to engage in another scrappy encounter with the delectable Melanie Winslow, but not today. "We're awfully busy right now, but..." He allowed a hint of a devilish smile to tug at the corners of his mouth. "I'm sure I could find some time to help her out."

Melanie stiffened at his teasing. "I don't require any help doing my job, thank you."

"Well, in case you have any questions that need to be answered, feel free to ask away."

Melanie definitely had some questions she wanted answered. Exactly how and where did Cody fit in? She wished she knew whether she could really trust him. She broke away from his mesmerizing pull, forcing her gaze out the window toward the delivery truck parked in front of the house.

Cody, too, returned his attention to the business at hand. "The delivery people are here with the hospital bed. The nurse that Doc Gerrard hired is also here. They want to get everything set up in the parlor." Cody looked past Melanie to where Buck rested in his bed, his eyes closed. He glanced back at Melanie, his voice lowered to a whisper. "Did Buck fall asleep? I really hate to wake him."

"No, Cody. I'm not sleeping, just resting my eyes." Buck's voice was still weak, but it sounded firmer than it had a few minutes earlier. "What's this about a nurse? I don't need a nurse."

Cody moved closer to Buck's bed. "You know what the doctor said. Now, for once, why don't you just put that stubborn streak of yours on hold and give it a try." The words were emphatic, but they could not hide the genuine warmth and affection Cody felt for Buck.

"Tell me, Cody—" Buck pretended a gruffness, but it was apparent he was joking as he acquiesced to Cody's decision about the nurse. "Just when was it that I lost control of the situation?"

Melanie thought back to the night before, to the bit of phone conversation she had overheard. Buck's comment, regardless of the fact that it was uttered in jest, elicited an entirely different reaction from her. Just when had Cody taken control of things and exactly how much control did he really have?

She glanced at her watch. It was still early. From her experience it was too early for an attorney to actually be in his office. She would wait another hour and then call Henry Sanderson.

Melanie replaced the phone receiver in the cradle. The conversation had been totally unsatisfactory. The secretary had informed her that Henry Sanderson had retired six years ago and that his son, Dennis Sanderson, had taken over the practice. That bit of information had been a disappointment to her, but the fact that Dennis had left early that morning on a business trip and would not be back for two days had left her out in the cold.

Too many things, too much confusion. Mel checked on her father. He appeared to be sleeping. She picked up the box containing her mother's journals and carried it to her bedroom. She set the carton on the floor next to her bed, reached inside to retrieve the top journal, then replaced it in the box. She decided to take them to her private retreat, where she could read without being disturbed. She headed toward the barn.

Melanie settled into the hayloft and opened the first journal. As she read the words, they manifested themselves in her head as her mother's voice. Buckminster Winslow had been thirty-two years old when he swept up the beautiful nineteen-year-old Virginia Faraday in a whirlwind courtship that resulted in their marriage one month later. He had taken her from the world of charity balls, gallery openings and symphony concerts to a cattle ranch in Colorado that he had inherited from his father.

He had told the young woman of gentle upbringing that ranching was sometimes a hard life, but his dream was to take the ranch and build it into something to be proud of, something to pass on to his children. Virginia's parents were not pleased with her choice of husband, especially with the difference in their ages, and were quite vocal in their disapproval of a cattle ranch in Colorado. Virginia had said that Buck Winslow was her husband and wherever he called home was where she would live.

Melanie's mother wrote of warmth, love and happiness. Her words spoke of shared moments, both joys and sorrows. The biggest sorrow had occurred three years before Melanie was born—the loss of what would have been her mother and father's first child.

Her mother had miscarried in her fourth month. Melanie had never known about the early pregnancy. The journals went on to tell of her father's constant attentions to her

mother as she fought the ensuing depression over the loss of
her first child. They painted a picture of a tender, caring and
loving man who himself had been deeply shaken by the loss,
yet saw to it that her mother wanted for nothing in the way
of emotional support and love.

Her mother's words continued to convey the hopes and
dreams of a husband and wife who desperately wanted another child, but as the time passed by it seemed that it was
not to be so. Then, when they had all but given up hope, her
mother became pregnant again. Both her parents were elated
at the news. Buck had wanted Virginia to go back East to
her home, to be with her family, where she would have the
proper surroundings of pampering and luxury during the
course of her pregnancy. He did not want her to take any
chances on complications developing. Virginia Winslow had
refused, saying the ranch was her home and her place was
there with her husband. The pregnancy had been a difficult
one. At one point her mother almost miscarried again.

Buck insisted that Virginia spend the eighth and ninth
months of her pregnancy confined to bed. He did everything, worked day and night to take care of the ranch and
the house and Virginia. Each night he would collapse into
bed totally exhausted, but never without kissing her good-
night and telling her how much he loved her.

The day after Melanie was born Buck went out and
bought Virginia a gold chain and locket, the locket Melanie
remembered her mother wearing every single day.

Melanie closed the journal. The tears flowed down her
cheeks and she was unable to hold back her sobs. She could
not read any more, not until she somehow managed to regain control of her emotions. She took several gulping
breaths, but they did not seem to help. If she was confused
before, then she was totally at a loss now.

Cody entered the barn. He was looking for Melanie, because Buck had been asking for her. The sounds of sobbing caught his attention. He glanced around the empty barn, then up toward the loft.

He climbed the ladder. The sight that greeted him tugged at his heartstrings. Melanie sat cross-legged in the hay, a cardboard box containing journals next to her. Her tear-stained cheeks added to the dazed look of bewilderment that covered her face. She clutched the journal against her chest as she stared blankly at the barn wall.

"Hey, are you all right?" His voice showed both surprise and a very real compassion.

She heard his words, knew he was there, but could not manage the energy required to answer him. She felt drained.

"Melanie?" A little hint of apprehension crept into his voice. She seemed so terribly distraught. He knew about the journals, knew Buck had been saving them for her, but had never actually seen them. He stepped off the top rung onto the loft floor, then he knelt down next to her. His voice softened. "Melanie?" He reached out to take the journal from her hand. "Are you okay?"

She tightened her grip on the notebook, refusing to relinquish it. She slowly turned her head in his direction and focused on his face. His features were soft, his expression showed a genuine concern. She forced her words, trying to keep the quaver out of her voice. "I'm fine. Thank you. I'll be okay."

He tugged at the journal, finally freeing it from her grasp. He placed it in the box with the others. He drew her into his embrace and held her body close to his. He felt the way she trembled, sensed her need for comfort. "You may be many things, but right now *fine* is not one of them."

Her need reached out to him and he responded by continuing to hold her tightly in his arms. He caressed her shoulders and occasionally leaned down and placed a soft kiss on her forehead, sometimes on her cheek. They stayed together in silence for several minutes. It was Cody who finally broke the shared silence. "Buck has been asking for you." He took a calming breath, then told her what he believed she needed to know. "His time is very short. He's starting to slip into what the doc called 'minicomas,' brief periods of time when he dozes off and literally forgets to breathe, then suddenly starts breathing again."

Melanie looked up at Cody, her eyes filled with tears. "Things I never knew...my mother miscarried...they lost a baby three years before I was born. My father was every bit as devastated as my mother. She almost miscarried again with me. He did everything by himself and insisted that she stay in bed and rest. I didn't know—" Her sobs cut off her words.

Cody was not sure what to do. He did not know if she had heard what he said. Doc Gerrard had told Cody what to expect. Buck would periodically doze off and simply forget to breathe for short instances of time. Those times would become more and more frequent until eventually he would not resume breathing, maybe another two or three days. Buck Winslow would die at home with dignity rather than hooked up to tubes and machines that served no purpose other than to monitor what was happening.

"Come on, Mel." He rose to his feet and reached for her arm to help her up. "Buck wants to see you. Do you want to leave these journals here or take them back to the house?"

She allowed him to help her up. She seemed bewildered by what he had said, momentarily lost in a cloud of uncertainty. "They're my mother's journals."

"I know. Buck told me about them."

"You've read my mother's journals?" Her brow knitted into a frown and her eyes narrowed, but not in time to prevent him from seeing the golden flecks of anger ignite. "How could you? They're private! They're her personal thoughts and feelings. My father saved them for me...only for me!"

He accepted her outburst and did not react to it, understanding that it had come from a very touchy place. "No, I've not read them. Buck told me they existed, that's all."

He bent to pick up the carton, hesitated a moment, then straightened again. He cupped her chin in his hand, lifted until her face was upturned, then brushed a gentle kiss across her lips. "I realize this has been very difficult for you. It wasn't at all what you expected." He placed another soft kiss on her cheek. "I know I haven't helped to make it any easier for you, either." He pulled her into his embrace. "I don't know what happened between you and your father, but I want you to know that he cares about you very much. He has only good things to say about you, never a negative word. He's very proud of you, Melanie. It clearly shows on his face every time he mentions your name."

Melanie allowed Cody to take the cardboard carton and escort her back to the house. They entered the parlor and quietly crossed to where Buck lay by the window. Cody set the carton next to the large easy chair by the bed. Buck appeared to be asleep, his breathing very shallow. At Cody's signal, the nurse unobtrusively slipped out of the room. He had indicated that Melanie would sit with her father for a while and the nurse could take a break.

Mel sank back into the softness of the large chair. She watched her father for a moment. The room was very still; the only sounds were her father's breathing. She looked up at Cody, her eyes saying what she could not say out loud—that she was very frightened about what was happening. As she looked away she felt his hand come down on her shoulder, followed by a little squeeze of comfort. She placed her hand on top of his.

"Uh, Cody." The voice containing a sense of urgency came from the door behind them and belonged to Ross Andrews. "Sorry to intrude, but it's Moonglow."

Cody gave Mel's shoulder another little squeeze. "I've got to get back to work. I'll talk to you later."

Cody and Ross left together, headed off toward the stables.

"She's dropping her foal. I've already put a call in to the vet. She's a few days early." Ross hurried on ahead of Cody.

Cody slowed his pace a bit as a series of thoughts darted through his mind. Things seemed to be coming together in such a strange and unexplainable way. Out of the blue, without even a hint of warning, Melanie Winslow had shown up as if in answer to Buck's silent prayers to be able to see his daughter once again. And now, even Moonglow was cooperating with an agenda that was clearly beyond the scope of mere mortals.

The mare was actually Moonglow II, granddaughter of the Arabian mare Buck had purchased for Melanie years ago. The first Moonglow had been born a month after Virginia died and Melanie departed for places unknown. Buck had been desperately trying to fight off the almost unbearable loneliness that had set in. He had named the foal Moonglow, after his wife's favorite song. Now Moonglow's grandchild would be here in time for Buck to see it. A new life entering the picture just as another life was about to exit.

Six

Several hours had passed since Ross Andrews had come looking for Cody, leaving Melanie alone with her father. She had remained in the chair next to her father's bed and silently sobbed as she read the rest of her mother's journals.

So many things she had never known. Her father had been absent at both her ninth and tenth birthdays. She remembered the hurt she had experienced when her mother had told her he would not be home to help her celebrate. She had been angry that he could not be bothered to spend that special evening with her, just one day out of the year. On her twelfth birthday he had bought her an Arabian mare of her very own, Lady Golden Dawn, but he had not been there to see her excitement. Now she understood—after all these years she now understood.

There had been a period when times had been very tough financially, a fact her parents had kept from her. Her father had been forced to take a night job in order to make ends meet. He worked all day on the ranch, then drove twenty-five miles one way to his night job. To have asked for the night off for her birthday would have cost him the job the family so desperately needed. Her mother wrote of his despair at not being able to celebrate with his daughter. And her horse—her father had sold his most priceless heirloom passed down to him by his father to get the money to buy her the horse.

All her life her father had seemed so unapproachable and gruff, too busy to have any time for her. She would try to get his attention and he would ignore her. Her mother's journals told of a man who loved his only child so much that sometimes when Melanie tried to talk to him he had to turn and walk away from her so that she would not see him choke up with emotion, would not see what he thought she would perceive as weakness.

She was shocked to read that it was really her father who had gone shopping for her first camera and who had proudly displayed her photographs to all their friends. All this time she had harbored a secret belief that her father had been seeing other women and that her mother's reluctance to discuss his nightly absences was because she was trying to shelter her daughter from the ugly truth. She had indeed been trying to shelter her daughter from the truth, but it was far from ugly. A jolt of shame and guilt shot through Melanie. All these years she had blamed her father for something that just was not true.

As she came to the end of the journals she read of the doctor saying that her mother did not have much time left. Her mother had made her father promise that he would not mention it to anyone, especially to their daughter. Buck had tried to get Virginia to go back to her family's home in the East or to at least let him hire someone to help her, but she refused. She said the ranch was her home and that was where she wanted to spend her final days, without a bunch of strangers hovering over her.

Her mother's final entry in her journal had been written the day she died.

Buck, I love you so very much. I see the tears in your eyes and hear the heartache in your voice. Please don't spend any sorrow at my passing. No woman could have asked for a more perfect life than you've given me. I ask only that you take care of Melanie and pass these journals on to her. Until we meet again, my love...

In the back of the last journal she found an envelope with her name on it. Her fingers trembled as she removed the delicate notepaper with the pale pink roses along the border. She was not sure how much more of this she could handle. She had already cried what seemed like a bucket of tears. The note was short.

My darling daughter,
By the time you read this I will no longer be with you, but I will always be watching over you. You have grown into a beautiful young woman with an exciting future ahead of you. I wish for you as much happiness in your life as I have been blessed with in my life. I want you to have this locket. I hope you treasure it as much as I have. I love you. Mother.

Melanie reached inside the envelope and withdrew the gold heart-shaped locket and chain her mother had always worn. Her fingers trembled as she opened the locket. Inside was a small photo depicting her mother and her father holding the newly born Melanie. The pride and love on her father's face were undeniable. She closed the locket, then fastened the chain around her neck.

She felt emotionally drained. It took all the effort she could muster to replace the final journal in the carton. She looked at her father sleeping peacefully. The man she had spent the first eighteen years of her life with had turned out to be a complete stranger. The man she thought she knew did not exist. She reached out and took his hand between her hands and held it there. He stirred slightly and slowly opened his eyes. As soon as he focused on her his eyes lit up and a smile turned the corners of his mouth.

"Mel, honey . . . I must have dozed off for a few minutes. Have you been sitting there long?" His voice was not strong, but it did not quaver as he spoke.

It had not been minutes—it had been hours. "Not too long. I . . . I've been reading Mother's journals." She felt the sob catch in her throat. Her hand automatically went to the locket around her neck. She moved from the chair to the edge of his bed. She busied herself for a few moments adjusting his blankets and pillow, using the time to pull together some sort of composure.

Her lip quivered as she tried to fight back her tears. She reached out and touched her trembling fingers to his cheek. She looked into his eyes and saw only love and devotion.

"I see you found Virginia's locket." He reached out and touched the heart-shaped ornament, then withdrew his hand. "I had planned to give it to you following the funeral, just as your mother had wanted me to do, but you . . ." He paused a moment, the emotion obviously overwhelming him. He swallowed a couple of times, then reached out again to touch the locket. "It looks real nice on you, honey."

She saw his eyes glisten. She could not hold back any longer. The tears streamed down her cheeks as she leaned forward and put her arms around him. The words gushed out in great sobs. "Oh, Daddy...so many things I never knew...I'm so very sorry."

Buck put his arms around his daughter. "Melanie. I'm so glad you've come home. I've missed you. It was almost more than I could bear, losing your mother and then a couple of days later losing you, too. I love you, honey. Maybe I never told you as much as I should have and I'm real sorry for that. I'd almost given up hope of ever seeing you again. I think I would have died long ago of loneliness if it hadn't been for Cody."

Cody again. Had he found in her father a vulnerable man who had just lost his family and was therefore ripe for the picking? She may have resolved her feelings about her father, but Cody Chandler was a totally different situation. She did not have the slightest idea how to reconcile the way he made her feel with what she suspected might be the truth about him.

She furrowed her brow in concentration for a moment. She had wrongly suspected the worst of her father and it had caused a huge rift between them that had lasted for years. Was she once again jumping to erroneous conclusions? Surely she had learned a very valuable lesson from all this, a lesson that she did not want to repeat.

"Buck—" Cody's voice held an unmistakable excitement as he rushed into the room. "We have a new foal and she's a real beauty. She has Moonglow's coloring and her classic Arabian lines." He concentrated his attention on Melanie for a moment. He made quick note of the way she sat on the edge of Buck's bed, her tear-stained face and puffy red eyes and the way she and her father seemed to cling to each other.

It was the first and only moment of true closeness he had witnessed between Melanie and her father. They both radiated an inner happiness that seemed to surround them in a loving glow. He hoped it meant what he thought it did, that whatever had caused the separation had somehow been patched up. Having his daughter back was all that Buck had wanted ever since Cody had known him. Perhaps Buck's wish had finally been granted.

Melanie saw her father's face light up at the news. He gave her hand a little squeeze; his eyes sparkled with excitement. "You hear that, Mel? The new foal—she's a direct line from your mare, honey. She's the great-granddaughter of Lady Golden Dawn, granddaughter of Moonglow and daughter of Moonglow II."

Melanie saw her father blink back some tears, heard the emotion in his words.

"Did you hear that, Melanie? She's a beautiful foal, just like her mother. Just like you, honey—beautiful...just like your mother."

Cody felt a warm inner glow as he watched Melanie and Buck. He was very pleased that his friend would now be able to truly rest in peace. It had jabbed at his conscience, this strong attraction he felt for Buck's daughter. He had been torn in two directions. On one hand, that first kiss told him he wanted her—how much and for what purpose had been unclear. On the other hand, there was his responsibility to his employer along with his genuine concern for his dear friend's anguish over the estrangement. His loyalties were with Buck, but his desires reached out for Melanie. Now the conflict seemed to have been resolved, leaving him with a clear path for a more aggressive pursuit of the intriguing Melanie Winslow.

"She's early. Moonglow dropped her foal early...." Buck's voice trailed off and a perplexed look crossed his face. "She wasn't due for another..." He shook his head in confusion. "I don't seem to remember."

Cody was at his side immediately. "Yes, she's a little early. She wasn't due for another four days yet. We have her up and walking around already. She's still not very steady, but the vet says she's strong and healthy. She's going to be just fine."

Buck sank back into the bed, a contented smile playing across his lips. "I'm a little tired right now. I'll go out to the stable first thing in the morning to see her." He looked up at Melanie, his gaze that of a doting father. "We'll both go out to the stable first thing in the morning, okay, honey?"

Melanie leaned forward and kissed him on the cheek. She stole a glance at Cody. She saw the sadness cover his features as he shook his head. She gave Buck a hug, then stood. "Of course, Daddy. We'll go first thing in the morning." She straightened his blankets. "You get some rest now. We'll talk later."

Melanie started across the room, then quickly turned and went back. Buck had fallen asleep. A cold shiver darted up her spine. Was the end nearly here? She watched him for a moment longer, then stooped to pick up the carton containing her mother's journals.

Cody was at her side in an instant. "Here, I'll take that." He took charge of the box. "Where do you want it to go?"

"I guess in my bedroom...." She felt the lump form in her throat. She swallowed a couple of times as she looked up at Cody.

He set the box on a table and pulled her into his arms. She offered no resistance as he cradled her head against his shoulder. He felt her body tremble, then she slipped her arms inside his jacket and around his waist. They held each other for several minutes, neither of them saying anything.

Finally Melanie broke away. She ran her fingers through her hair and nervously brushed at her jeans and tugged at her sweater. Cody's embrace had made her feel more at ease with what was happening, but very ill at ease about her feelings for him. He seemed to instinctively know when she needed a hug, a moment of extra solace, some additional comfort. She was beginning to see why her father was so fond of him. She was also beginning to realize that she was growing very fond of him, too—perhaps too fond for her own good.

"I'll be okay." She picked up the carton from the table. "I can take this. I'm sure you have lots of work to do, things that require your attention."

Cody escorted her as far as her bedroom door. "Are you sure you're going to be okay?" His concern was genuine. She had obviously been through an emotional upheaval. He wanted to help her, wanted to make the next few days as painless for her as possible. He did not know what had been in her mother's journals, but whatever it was it had brought about a miraculous change in her attitude toward her father.

He bent forward, brushed his lips against hers, then moved in for a more intimate kiss. His mouth lingered, and once again he tasted the sweetness that was uniquely hers— the sweetness that beckoned him onward. He reluctantly pulled back from her, traced her jaw with his fingertip, then turned to leave. "I'll see you later."

She watched as Cody disappeared down the hallway. She took in a deep breath, then slowly let it out. It did not help. Her insides still quivered with excitement. She wished she knew more about him. Where did he come from? How had he earned his living before going to work for her father? What was someone with his type of educational background doing working as a ranch hand?

The night air was crisp and saturated with the fragrance of wildflowers combined with a scent that foretold of rain.

Melanie zipped up her jacket as she walked toward the stables. She had spent the rest of the afternoon and early evening with her father. He appeared to tire easily. Sometimes they would talk and other times she would sit as he napped. She could tell he was pushing himself to the limit to carry on a conversation with her.

They talked about so many things, each making an effort to pack a lifetime into what little time was left to them. When he dozed off again the nurse suggested Melanie let him sleep the rest of the night, that the excitement was taking too much of a toll on his strength.

Melanie spotted Cody as she entered the stables. She went directly to Moonglow's stall, stepped inside and closed the gate behind her. "So, this is the new foal." Melanie reached out and stroked Moonglow's neck as she watched the foal try to steady herself on her long, wobbly legs. "She's certainly a beautiful little girl." She glanced up at Cody. "Does she have a name yet?"

"Yes, she does. Buck chose it earlier this evening, while you were having dinner." He studied her for a moment. She seemed much more composed. Her eyes were no longer red and puffy, her cheeks no longer streaked with tears. He felt a tightening in his chest, an involuntary reaction to his attempt to quell his very real urge to carry her off to the hayloft and make love to her.

She cocked her head and arched an eyebrow. "Well?" When he did not immediately respond she offered a warm smile. "Aren't you going to tell me what it is?"

"Ah...yes. The name." He shook away his errant thoughts, or at least he attempted to shake them away. To his exasperation, they refused to leave his head. The dim night lighting in the stables highlighted her delicate features. The tilt of her nose, the thrust of her chin, the way each breath she drew resulted in the gentle rise and fall of the curve of her breasts beneath her sweater—everything about her excited his senses. He took her hand in his and pulled her to him.

She experienced a shortness of breath. Once again he had sent her common sense into a tailspin. She fought to get out the words. "The name... the foal's name..."

"Buck named her *Melanie's Homecoming.*"

Before she could say anything, he captured her mouth with a demanding kiss. He nibbled at the corners of her lips, then slid his mouth fully onto hers. She was softness, sweetness and heated sensuality all rolled up into one very desirable package.

He pulled her body tight against his. A moment later he felt her arms encircle him, then her hands slide across the back of his jacket as she returned his embrace. Her response was at first hesitant but quickly escalated to match his level of excitement. At that moment she was everything he had ever wanted. He probed the warm, dark recesses of her mouth with his tongue, tasting the hidden treats and delights he knew he would find there.

Melanie readily accepted the thrust of his tongue, the sensation of the texture brushing against hers. She quickly lost herself in the aura of sexual magnetism that surrounded him and deftly reached out to ensnare her. She reached her arms up around his neck, then ran her fingers through his thick, blond hair.

In a split second Cody realized that Moonglow had moved around behind him, but it was too late. The mare placed her head against his back and gave him a gentle shove. He tumbled to the floor of the stall, pulling Melanie down with him. Whatever thoughts he had about where their heated moment might have led them were buried in a pile of straw and a cloud of dust when he landed with a thud and she fell on top of him.

Moonglow snorted at them, as if to say, *This is my room. Go find a place of your own.* Her foal kicked up her back legs and followed her mother to the other side of the large stall.

Cody made no attempt to get up. Quite the contrary, he wiggled his body down into the hay and held Melanie tightly on top of him. With one arm wrapped around her shoulders and the other hand gliding smoothly across the denim covering the curve of her bottom cheek, he brushed a soft kiss against her lips. His voice was husky, yet conveyed just enough of a teasing quality to prevent her from being alarmed. "Animals are very instinctual about these things and it seems that Moonglow has her own suggestion about what we should be doing. What do you think?"

Melanie almost had her soaring hormones under control...almost. A warm tingle spread through her body when his lips grazed hers. The feel of his hard frame against hers sent waves of desire right to her innermost core. "I think—"

His tongue teased that tender spot behind her ear, then she felt his teeth gently nibble at her earlobe. His warm breath whispered in her ear. "You think what?" Before she could answer, he again captured her mouth with an earthy kiss that spoke volumes about the sensuality of the man.

Melanie knew in a heartbeat that the harmless little flirtation had evolved into something much more serious, something very real. At least it had for her. Was it nothing more than an amusing pastime for Cody? She broke off the kiss. Her breathing was ragged. "I think we should stop this before it's too late." She wished she really believed the words she had just said, the truth being that stopping was the last thing she truly wanted.

"Before it's too late for what?" His breathing was every bit as ragged as hers. The flame in her eyes and the sight of her kiss-swollen lips pulled at his senses. He knew the wisdom of her words, but it did nothing to alter what he felt.

She struggled to her feet. She tried not to look at Cody lying back in the hay. She could not answer his question. She brushed the dust from her clothes. Her voice held a nervous edge to it. "I want to check on Daddy, make sure he's comfortable."

Cody looked up at her, grabbing her gaze and holding it for a moment with his own, then rose to his feet. He plucked a couple of pieces of straw from her hair. His words were soft, and unmistakably sincere. "I wish you had come back a long time ago."

She flicked some dirt from the shoulder of his shirt, the intimate exchange of gestures not lost on either of them. "So do I." She nervously cleared her throat and took a step back in an attempt to distance herself from his all-too-tempting closeness. "I've missed so much time that I could have spent with my father." That was not the only thing she had missed out on. She briefly wondered what would have happened if she had met Cody eight years ago, when he first came to the ranch.

"Yeah . . . of course." That had not been what Cody had in mind. His thoughts were of a much more personal nature. He leaned against the railing separating the stalls and watched as she left the stables and walked back toward the house.

Melanie Winslow was becoming more and more important to him with each passing minute. But the future was uncertain—Buck's remaining time could be as short as a couple of days. After that there would be the legal loose ends to be tied neatly together, even though Buck had already made out a will and put his business affairs in order. Cody wondered if his interest in Melanie would be considered disloyal to Buck. It was a dilemma that had intruded into his thoughts a lot in the past twenty-four hours. Melanie Winslow was a beautiful and vibrant woman who, whether he liked it or not, literally set his soul on fire.

Melanie poured a cup of coffee and stood at the kitchen window, watching for a moment as the early-morning sun broke through the clouds. She had already checked on her father. The nurse said he had spent a peaceful night and was resting easy.

So many things filled Melanie's mind. The one thought that had caught her off guard was what it would be like to live on the ranch again. It was just about the last thing she would ever have considered, but now things were different. So much had changed in the past couple of days. Things were no longer clear-cut.

"Good morning."

Cody's voice sent a little tremor of excitement through her body as he came up behind her. She had tried not to think about him. It had not worked. She had been determined not to dream about him. That, too, had been futile. The little tremor inside her quickly became much more when he slipped his arms around her waist, nuzzled his face against her hair, then kissed the side of her neck.

She twisted in his arms until she had turned around to face him. She made a gallant effort to sound casual. "Good morning yourself." A moment later his mouth was on hers, rekindling all the heated desires from the night before. The kiss did not last long, but the meaning ran deep—at least it did for Melanie. Cody still represented a puzzle to her. He obviously liked touching her and kissing her, but was that all it was to him? Just some type of amusing game to be put away on the closet shelf when it no longer amused?

"What do you have planned for the day?" He pressed his body against hers, leaning her back against the kitchen counter. Her nearness was intoxicating. Her warmth penetrated right through his clothes and suffused him with a feeling of contentment. The selfish, immature, unfeeling woman he had imagined Melanie to be simply did not exist. He had never met anyone quite like her. Did he dare give any credence to the word *love?*

"I thought I would go horseback riding for a bit. Maybe head west toward the box canyon, take my cameras and do some photography for my magazine article." She wanted some time alone, some time to think things through without any distractions—and Cody Chandler was a gigantic distraction if ever there was one. She was acutely aware of the way he had skillfully maneuvered their positions so that his body snuggled neatly against hers—and a perfect fit it was, too.

Their conversation continued soft and intimate, each experiencing an increasingly heightened sense of longing and closeness. After several minutes Cody straightened up, breaking the physical contact between them. "I'd love to go riding with you—"

That was not at all what Melanie wanted. Cody was one of the things she needed to think about. She was about to interject, making some excuse to decline his offer, but realized that it would not be necessary.

"But I have a very busy day." He settled an affectionate kiss on her cheek. What was there about this woman that had so totally captivated him? Why was he unable to keep his hands off her? Perhaps fate had stepped in to take matters out of his hands, to put some type of restraint on things before they escalated completely out of his control. He brushed a loose tendril of hair away from her cheek, then tucked it behind her ear. "Ross can saddle a horse for you. Make sure you take some water with you and—"

"Hey... I grew up here, remember?" She chided him, but this time it was done in a teasing manner rather than with anger.

A sheepish grin turned the corners of his mouth when he realized how silly his instructions must have sounded. "Right. I've lived here several years and you've only been here a few days. I guess I forgot this was your home before it was mine. I'll see you when you get back."

There it was again, his proprietary attitude about her father's ranch. Something else she needed to think about, to figure out.

Melanie gathered her things, slung her bag over her shoulder and headed toward the stables in search of Ross Andrews. After she assured him her riding skills were top rate, he selected a spirited quarter horse named Proud Warrior for her use.

Cody watched from the office window as she rode off toward the foothills. Everything about her excited him right down to his toes. He allowed a heavy sigh, then situated himself in front of the computer. He stared at the monitor screen, but did not put his fingers on the keyboard. There were several things on his mind, not the least of which was what to do about Melanie Winslow.

He had refused to clearly define his feelings about her. He feared exactly what those feelings might be. He had a responsibility to Buck and to the running of the ranch. He did not know just how a personal relationship with Buck's daughter would fit into that picture. With great difficulty he forced his mind away from Melanie Winslow and to the work that required his attention.

Seven

Melanie sat on a large rock next to a clear stream. The snowmelt rushed fast and cold out of the mountains. She munched on a bite of apple as she scanned the horizon. The gathering of clouds had turned from fluffy white to dark and ominous. What had been a refreshing breeze just an hour earlier had turned cool and brisk. The smell of rain saturated the air.

She stood up, brushed the dirt from the seat of her jeans and grabbed her jacket. She gave the rest of her apple to Proud Warrior, then shrugged into her jacket. She should have started back toward the ranch house as soon as the clouds turned ugly.

Her horse snorted and pawed at the ground. The approaching storm made him nervous. Melanie picked up her bag, packed everything back inside and zipped it shut. She put the strap over her head and across one shoulder so that the bag rested comfortably across her body for the ride back. She placed her left foot in the stirrup and started to swing her right leg up and over.

Sometimes the smallest of things could spook a horse—a tree branch swaying erratically in the wind, a bird's wings flapping in the brush. This was one of those times. Proud Warrior bolted and ran, throwing Melanie to the ground.

Cody had been in the office since Melanie departed on horseback for the far reaches of the ranch. It was now late afternoon. His shoulders and back ached from sitting in the chair, hunched over the computer for so long. He stood and stretched out the kinks from his body. He needed to check on things outside, but first he wanted to look in on Buck. The nurse assured him that Buck had spent a relatively comfortable day, much of it napping. Cody reached the front door just in time to see Ross bounding up the porch steps.

"Cody... Miss Winslow's horse just came back to the corral without her."

"What?" An adrenaline charge pumped hard through his chest and Cody came off the porch like a shot. "What happened?" He felt a cold tremor of foreboding settle in the pit of his stomach.

"I don't know. She came to me this morning sayin' she wanted to go riding. Told me she was a good rider and wanted a horse with some spirit, so I saddled up Proud Warrior for her. He's a good horse, handles well and could give her a fast ride if that's what she wanted."

Cody's fast-paced walk turned into a run as he headed toward the stables. "Did she say anything? Give you any clue where she intended to go?"

Ross was having a difficult time keeping up with Cody's long legs as he hurried along beside him. "She mentioned the box canyon and asked if the trapper's cabin was still there."

"Damn." Cody paused for a moment, his brow wrinkled in thought. "The four-wheel drive won't do me any good if I have to go up into the canyon. Saddle my horse while I grab some supplies."

Ross went one direction and Cody went another.

Cody picked up a small first-aid kit and a cellular phone from the communications office. Next he went into the supply room and packed a large high-intensity flashlight, extra batteries and a couple of rain ponchos into saddlebags. On his way out the door he pulled two heavy jackets from the rack and wrapped them in a plastic sheet, one for him and the other for Melanie.

Cody headed his horse west, straight out across the pasture toward the foothills. He kept a wary eye on the black storm clouds moving in over the hills. He judged that maybe an hour of decent daylight was left, depending on how quickly the storm closed in around him.

He kept telling himself that Melanie was all right. Something had spooked her horse, but she was resourceful and self-sufficient. Besides, she grew up on the ranch. Even though it had been a while, she would still know her way around. If she was anywhere near the old trapper's cabin, she would be safe.

That was what he kept telling himself. He would say the words over and over again, sometimes in his mind and sometimes out loud. It was more than just Buck's daughter who was out there somewhere; it was the woman...

Cody could not finish the thought, did not want to finish it. He was afraid to finish it. He had been able to shove it from his mind because there was always a convenient excuse close at hand for diverting his attention to other matters. Now there were no interruptions to turn his thoughts elsewhere. Melanie Winslow was the only thing on his mind.

Raindrops splattered on the brim of his hat, first gently, then with more force. Cody reached back and extracted one of the rain ponchos from the saddlebag. It was going to be a wet evening, but he was determined not to stop until he located Melanie.

He turned north along the stream, headed toward the box canyon. Two hours had passed since it started raining, even though it seemed much longer to him. In another fifteen minutes he would be at the trapper's cabin, and if he was lucky his search would be over. He bowed his head, allowing some of the collected water to run off his hat brim. He continued along the stream bank, trying not to dwell on the other possibilities.

Cody blinked a couple of times in an attempt to clear away the rain that partially obscured his vision. Through the gloom and wet he could make out a dim light around the edges and through the cracks of the shuttered window. The wet night air carried the smell of wood burning in the fireplace. Someone was in the cabin. The excitement built inside him as he urged his horse into a faster gait.

He jumped off his horse in front of the cabin, landing in a muddy puddle. He clasped the reins in one hand and grasped the door latch with the other. It was secured from the inside. He banged with his fist. "Melanie! Are you in there? Open up. It's Cody." A moment later the door opened.

"This is a surprise." It may have been an impish grin that turned the corners of her mouth, but it was not light-hearted amusement that she had initially felt when she heard someone at the door. At the sound of Cody's voice an immediate feeling of relief settled over her. "What are you doing here, cowboy? Did you just happen to be in the neighborhood and thought you'd stop by to say hello?"

What was at one time probably an expensive Stetson was now soaking wet, with the brim hanging low over his forehead. The bright-yellow rain poncho covered him from his shoulders almost to his knees. His jeans and boots were mud spattered from the bottom of the poncho to the ground. To Melanie's eyes he looked gorgeous. Before she was able to move aside so that he could come in out of the rain, he impulsively grabbed her. He pulled her outside the cabin and enfolded her in his arms as if he had not heard a word she said.

The cold rain hit against her back. His wet poncho soaked through the front of her clothes. The brim of his hat hit against her forehead as he pulled her into his embrace.

"Are you all right, Mel? You're not hurt, are you?" He tightened his hold on her, crushing her body against his.

The way he had her head buried against his shoulder prevented her from answering him right away. Despite the cold rain that pounded down on them, a warm feeling flowed through her body.

He finally released her from his embrace but continued to grip her shoulders with his hands. He held her in front of him, his eyes telling her how much he cared, even if his words had not. At least, that was what she hoped they were saying.

A bit of a calm settled over Cody. The rain did not matter; the mud did not matter. The important thing was that she had apparently escaped unharmed. He repeated his question. "Are you okay?"

"Do you mean other than the fact that I was dry and now I'm very wet?" Melanie could not stop the teasing grin that spread across her face. "Yes, I'm fine—except for this sprained ankle."

He glanced down and saw that she was standing on the muddy step, not wearing her boots, and seemed to be favoring her right ankle.

The air surrounding them may have been cold and wet, but the energy that flowed between them was undeniably hot. He cupped her chin in his hand and lifted her face upward. The rain splattered on her cheeks and forehead. He lowered his head, his mouth seeking out hers. His horse tugged at the reins still clutched in his other hand, reminding him there were immediate considerations that needed tending to. The intimate moment of tenderness had been broken. He allowed a sigh of resignation, then satisfied himself with a quick brush of his lips against hers.

Cody physically turned her toward the door. "Get back inside out of the rain. There's no way we're going to try making it to the house tonight, not riding double in this storm. I'm going to bed my horse down in the lean-to next to the cabin. I'll be right back."

Mel stepped inside the cabin, favoring her right ankle as she moved away from the door. A cold chill shivered through her body, probably caused by her wet clothes. She limped over to the fireplace to warm herself. She stared at the fire, allowing herself to be drawn into the mesmerizing rhythm of the flames dancing across the logs. Perhaps the shiver was due not so much to her wet clothes as to the possibilities the night held.

Cody struggled through the cabin door. He clutched the saddle horn in one hand, with the saddle slung across his shoulder and back. In his other hand he carried the saddlebags. He kicked the door shut with a muddy boot as he swung the saddle off his shoulder and set it on the plank floor. He carried the saddlebags to the other side of the small, one-room cabin and placed them on the table. He clamped his teeth onto a fingertip of his rugged leather glove

and worked his hand free. He tugged the other glove off and
dropped both of them on the table. He pulled the wet poncho over his head and hung it on the wall peg, the water
dripping to the floor. His final chore before turning his attention to Melanie was to shake the rain from his hat and set
it on the table next to the saddlebags and gloves.

"Now..." He ruffled his fingers through his damp hair.
"You say you're perfectly fine? The way you're favoring
that ankle says you are *not* perfectly fine."

Her ankle throbbed as she tried to put her full weight on
it. "It's nothing. I had stopped by the stream for lunch. The
dark clouds began to look pretty ominous and I realized I
needed to start back. Just as I was mounting my horse
something spooked him. He reared, threw me to the ground
and took off. I was less than a quarter mile from the cabin
and figured it would give me some shelter from the storm. I
found a tree branch to use as a sort of makeshift crutch. It
was a little tricky walking here, but I made it just as it started
to rain."

"You seem to be very resourceful and coolheaded in a
crisis."

"Thank you." She glanced shyly at the floor, then added
as an afterthought, "I assume the horse is okay, that he went
back to the stables on his own."

"Yes, Proud Warrior showed up in time for dinner."
Cody glanced around the interior of the cabin. Not only had
she lit the kerosene lantern and built a fire in the fireplace,
she had opened one of the stockpiled cans of soup and
heated it on the grate. "I see you found everything okay. We
keep this cabin stocked with emergency provisions for situ-
ations just like this. There have been numerous occasions
when some of the hands have been out riding the fence line,
looking for breaks, and have used it overnight so they could
continue the next morning without having to go all the way

back to the bunkhouse." A hint of a teasing grin tugged at the corners of his mouth. "It's even been used as shelter from a sudden storm."

"Well, whoever came up with that plan certainly gets my vote. I can't tell you how relieved I was to find firewood and matches. The lantern and canned goods on the shelf were an added plus." Melanie hobbled over to the table, seated herself in one of the chairs and put her foot up on the other chair in an effort to elevate her ankle. She watched as Cody removed his jacket and hung it on the wall peg next to his wet poncho.

She closed her eyes for a moment and allowed her thoughts to fill her consciousness. It all seemed so *civilized.* He had stated and she had silently agreed that they would spend the night together in the cabin. Other than that moment he had grabbed her and pulled her into his arms at the door, everything had been so proper, so polite, so business-like . . . so *civilized.*

Those thoughts did not last long. A moment later she felt his warm breath across her cheek, then his lips on the side of her neck. Her insides melted into a simmering pool of desire. His words tickled across her ear.

"I'll check in with Ross, then we'll see to your ankle . . . and figure what to do about tonight."

His last words touched far more than her desires.

He pulled the cellular phone from the saddlebag and dialed. A moment later he tried to carry on a conversation, but to no avail.

"Ross? I can barely hear you. You're breaking up. Just listen. I found her. She's okay. We're at the trapper's cabin. We'll stick it out here tonight. How's—" He stared at the dead phone, then turned it off and set it on the table. "The storm seems to be interfering with reception. The call disconnected before I could ask about Buck."

Cody lifted her leg from the chair so he could sit down, then rested her leg across his thigh. He peeled off her wet, muddy sock. "Now, let's take a look at this ankle." It was noticeably swollen and some bruising had already set in. "Does this hurt?" He gently rotated her foot, mindful of the pained wince that briefly contorted her features. He was also very aware of the way her neatly pedicured toes with the russet-colored polish peeked through the muddy film that covered her foot. "Sorry, I'll try to be more careful." He turned up the hem of her jeans until the cuff was almost to her knee. "We need to get this wrapped and you should stay off it as much as possible."

He retrieved the first-aid kit from the saddlebag. He took out an elastic bandage and expertly wrapped her ankle. "There, that should do it for now." He looked up and caught her gaze.

The captivating pull of his masculinity held her to him. She tried to concentrate on what was happening and not think about the night ahead of them. She felt his fingers glide up her bare shin, then back down her calf. He paused a moment, then carefully lowered her foot to the floor. A huskiness enveloped his words, a huskiness that he could not hide. "Does the bandage feel okay? It's not too tight, is it? We'll have the nurse look at that ankle tomorrow."

She stood and carefully tested her weight on it, then took a couple of steps before returning to her chair. "It feels fine." Her words contained the same husky edge that his did. "Thanks for wrapping it for me."

No electricity, no running water other than what rushed along the stream bed, no luxuries of any type, yet Melanie had never felt so pampered. She had been witness to the aggressive way he took charge of things, seen his ruggedness and experienced the magic of his sensuality firsthand. But this display of tenderness and gentle care had surprised her.

She studied the intensity in his face, accentuated by the clear blue honesty of his eyes. There had been no hint that anything more intimate than what had already happened would present itself. But if that was so, then how come her heart raced and a million butterflies darted around inside her stomach?

Cody leaned forward in his chair and pulled off one boot, dropping it to the floor with a thud. He repeated the process with the other boot, then set both of them in front of the fireplace so they could dry.

He added a couple more logs to the blaze. "I suppose we should see about some sleeping arrangements." He did not look at her. Instead he poked at the fire with an old branding iron he found next to the fireplace. He was not happy with the nervousness that jittered just below the surface of his skin.

Everything up until now had been casual and open. Melanie had been free to walk away from him at any time if she so chose. But this was different. Weather, darkness, the isolated location, her sprained ankle—she was not free to walk away tonight. Would she feel pressured by him if he pursued his desires? She scorched his very soul the way no other woman ever had, an admission he was reluctant to make even to himself.

Even though it had been nine years ago, the very intense affair he had had with an ambitious young woman in New York still haunted him. He had mistakenly thought he was in love. Instead, he had learned a valuable lesson. He could not get out of New York City fast enough. He wanted to get as far removed from the life-style of big city and bright lights as possible, from shallow people and money-grubbing fortune hunters. Love…he was not even sure he knew what the word meant anymore.

He needed to keep busy, keep his mind from gravitating to very real thoughts of what the night might bring—to very real feelings about Melanie Winslow. He nervously cleared his throat. "There should be some sleeping bags in the cupboard. I see you have one of the cots set up. There should be another one folded away with the sleeping bags."

Melanie was distinctly aware of the awkwardness surrounding them. *All right Ms. I-can-take-care-of-myself-and-don't-need-anybody, what do you plan to do now?* This was not a time to panic. She was a self-sufficient, capable woman who would handle this logically and intelligently. At least, that was what she told herself. Levelheaded thinking was definitely in order, not irresponsible behavior.

She watched as he tended the fire. He jabbed the burning logs, causing embers to fly, the same type of hot sparks she felt every time he kissed her. Maybe common sense and levelheaded thinking were not all they were cracked up to be.

"There." Cody replaced the branding iron next to the fireplace. "That should take care of things for a while." He did not look at her, choosing to turn his attention to sleeping bags and cots, instead. He should have sent Ross to find her. Or maybe he should have sent Edna to find her. He should have sent both Ross and Edna. Perhaps he should have called the sheriff's department. Anything would have been better than this.

He unfolded the second cot and set it next to the wall, purposely positioning it on the other side of the room from the one she had set up for herself. He located four sleeping bags, unrolling two of them and placing them on the cots. He took the other two and completely unzipped them so they would lay flat like a couple of quilts. He put one on top of the other on the floor in front of the fireplace. He stared into the flames. He had finished all the busy work and it had not helped one bit. Melanie Winslow was still the foremost thing on his mind.

He extinguished the wick on the lantern, leaving only the fireplace to provide both illumination and heat. He sat on the opened sleeping bags in front of the fire. He felt the bottoms of his pant legs. His wet jeans had started to dry. He nervously cleared his throat, then finally looked up at Melanie sitting in the chair. Her hair had almost dried. She had fluffed it with her fingers so that it feathered around her face. He had tried to ignore what was going on inside him, to not think about what the night would bring. He had not succeeded. "There didn't seem to be much reason to burn up the kerosene." He cleared his throat again.

The circumstances were ripe for seduction. Stranded overnight in a cabin, romantic fire, the sound of rain falling on the roof—the only things missing were soft music and a bottle of fine wine. Cody was not accustomed to dealing with nervousness and uncertainty in anything, and that definitely included his encounters with women—both personal and business. So why did he feel so ill at ease?

He was not the only one experiencing the unsettling pull of the surroundings. Melanie had watched the strong, fluid movements of his body as he worked. A mental image of his bare chest and arms, of his hard, taut body, kept popping into her mind—the image that had become stored there the night he had tackled her to the floor.

She wanted to remove the image from her mind and also erase the thoughts that went with it. She rose from the chair and moved carefully toward the fireplace, being protective of her injured ankle. "My clothes are still damp. I'd better get closer to this fire if I expect them to dry sometime soon." She knew how inane the words sounded, but the quiet was making her even more nervous.

She stood facing the fire, holding her hands out in front of her in order to warm them. She slowly turned around, her eyes immediately locking with his. "This is silly, isn't it?" She could barely force out the words. "I mean . . . are you feeling as uncomfortable and awkward as I am?"

He leaned back on one elbow, his long legs stretched out in front of him. "I was until just now." He did not take his eyes off her. In fact, he could not take his eyes off her. The golden glow of the fireplace spread across the floor, growing dimmer as it reached outward until it disappeared into the shadows at the corners of the room. He held his hand out toward her. "Come on, sit down here with me. I think we should talk . . . truly get acquainted."

She could hardly breathe. It was almost as if the fireplace were sucking in all the oxygen and carrying it up the chimney with the smoke. "Yes . . ." She hesitated for a brief instant before moving toward him. "I suppose we should get to know each other better. You seem to already know quite a bit about me." She seated herself on the laid-out sleeping bags. "It appears that everybody already knows quite a bit about me." The words were not said in anger or with animosity toward the fact that she had obviously been a frequent topic of conversation around the ranch.

"Not really. Buck is very proud of you, of what you've accomplished. That's all. Maybe Edna and I know a little more than that, but no one else." Cody leaned back on both elbows and stared at the flames in a reflective manner. A warm smile turned the corners of his mouth as the memories came to the forefront. "I remember the first time he came across one of your articles in a magazine. It was a little over six years ago. You should have seen him. He was so excited. You would have thought he had just won a million-dollar lottery." He shifted his gaze to her. "It was the one about the bush pilots in Alaska. You captured some truly spectacular pictures." He sat upright, reached out and gently brushed his fingertips across the side of her face, then brought them to rest beneath her chin. "You're a very talented photographer."

"Thank you. It's something I've always enjoyed." She felt the flush come to her cheeks. "That was my first spread in a major magazine." She glanced at the floor, her eyes downcast in embarrassment, then slowly looked up again to find his steady gaze still on her.

A comfortable warmth filled the room. It was a radiance far more intense than the heat that emanated from the fireplace. Melanie saw that same warmth in Cody's eyes and it touched a very vulnerable place deep inside her.

She had never allowed herself to become emotionally involved before, at least not to the extent where things might have taken that final step and turned into love. When a relationship became too emotionally intimate, she always managed to find some excuse to break it off. She usually blamed it on her job, saying she was away too much to devote the time required to maintain a relationship. When the moment came to face up to her own fears and insecurities she would end up running just as she had her entire adult life—starting with the day of her mother's funeral.

Perhaps that was why she had returned to the ranch. She was tired of running. It was time to confront those fears and overcome those insecurities. When her mother died she had feared that no one else would ever love her, certainly not her father, who had always been so cold and remote. Her decision to return to the ranch had brought her full circle. The love she thought she had lost for all time when her mother died had been found again in a father who had always loved her and had not stopped when she ran away, leaving him at a time when he needed her the most.

And now here was this man. Cody Chandler aroused desires, needs and wants in her the way no one else ever had.

The rain pounded down harder against the roof. The sound of the wind howled through the trees. The fire crackled and popped in the fireplace. Melanie pulled back slightly, breaking the physical contact of his fingers under her chin. "What about you? Where did you come from? How did someone who speaks fluent French and German and has a master's degree in philosophy end up working on a cattle ranch?"

Cody stretched out on his back with his hands behind his head. He pondered the question for a moment, not sure how to answer it. "Well, I was born in Connecticut. My father worked in banking and thought I should do the same, so he *encouraged* me to get a degree in finance. I decided that something in international banking might be more interesting and also present some travel opportunities. I learned French and German with an eye to the possibility of eventually ending up in Switzerland." A career in banking was what his father had wanted for him, what he had insisted on. Richard C. Chandler, Jr., had planned for his son to go into the family business. He was grooming his only heir to take over the family financial holdings, which were quite extensive and varied.

The only problem with his father's blueprint for the future was that Richard C. Chandler III wanted no part of the family empire. He was so determined to distance himself from East Coast society life that he began using his middle name—Cody.

"I kept telling myself that I could adapt to the world of high finance, but I really didn't like banking all that much. I guess the degree in philosophy came about as a result of trying to—" he paused, a slight chuckle escaping his throat "—to *find* myself." He rolled over on his side to face her, propping his head with his hand. He had not been prepared for the touch of embarrassment caused by his own words. "Oh, Lord." Another chuckle stopped his words for a moment. "That sounds really ridiculous... doesn't it?"

He had not intended to reveal so much about his past, but being cloistered in one small room with Melanie Winslow for the duration of the night had created an atmosphere of closeness and sharing that he had not anticipated. He rather enjoyed the unexpected happening. He did not have anyone he was truly close to anymore on a personal level. No one, that is, expect Buck and Edna, who had functioned as a surrogate family for him for the past eight years. Certainly not his own family, which was composed of his father and some obscure aunts, uncles and cousins.

Even though he had been hard on Melanie about her estrangement from her father, he fully understood dysfunctional families. He came from one. It still galled his father that Cody's grandmother had set up a trust fund for him, thereby diverting a healthy chunk of the family fortune away from his father. He could read it between the lines in every letter his father sent him and in every phone conversation they had... both occurrences becoming fewer and fewer with each passing year. In fact, their primary communication these days was through lawyers, profit and loss statements and an occasional e-mail via computer.

Eight

Cody seemed to be allowing her a glimpse into a vulnerability Melanie never suspected might exist with such a self-assured, strong-willed man. "And did you?" She lost her train of thought for an instant as the mesmerizing pull of his presence tugged at her reality. "Uh... that is, did you find yourself?"

Cody studied Melanie, her delicate features bathed in the soft light from the fireplace. He was not accustomed to talking about his background. His normal attitude was that it was no one's business. But their conversation had moved to a personal level, one that had turned surprisingly comfortable. It had become a time of sharing. The period of challenging and testing each other had passed. "Not right away. Not for a few years. Not until I left New York and headed west." Was he getting in over his head? He refused to admit that he was probably already there. He ran his finger across the back of her hand. He liked the feel of her skin, so soft and smooth. Then he laced their fingers together in an intimate gesture.

She curled her fingers around his. "Why did you decide to work on a ranch? That seems pretty far removed from banking." He had said they should talk, get to know each other better, but this was much more than she had anticipated. She had assumed *getting to know each other* meant he would ask all the questions and expect her to come up with all the answers.

It was a strange turn of events. Here they were, just the two of them, all alone for the entire night. He certainly had not exhibited any qualms about pulling her into his arms and kissing her senseless on previous occasions, so why not now? Instead he seemed to be orchestrating an unhurried journey toward true intimacy, a path paved with genuine affection and respect that allowed them to move forward on solid footing.

"I like the open spaces, the fresh air and the honesty of the land. It's a life-style without pretenses." He pulled her toward him and enfolded her in his arms. He threaded his fingers through her hair until he had the back of her head cradled in his hand. "I've found what I was seeking." He searched the depths of her eyes. "At least most of it." He leaned his face into hers and placed a tender kiss on her lips. "How about you, Mel? What is it you're searching for?"

"I don't know. Maybe I was trying to get back to basics, too. I suppose you could say I was looking for my roots." His face was so close to hers, their lips almost touching as they talked. "Whatever it was, I felt I needed to make contact with my father again."

"You've given Buck the one thing he wanted above all else, the one thing that made him the happiest—to see his daughter again. I'm glad you did, for Buck's sake as well as yours." A throaty emotion clung to his whispered words. "I'm glad for my sake, too."

He rolled her body over on top of his as he caressed her shoulders and back. He ran his fingers through her hair, tasted the tender spot behind her ear, then gently tugged at her earlobe with his teeth. He was not sure how far to take things, how far she would allow him to take their intimacy. He did know that he wanted much more than an embrace and a kiss. But how much more? A one-time roll in the hay? A relationship? A commitment?

Melanie did not wait for Cody to find her mouth. She sought out his lips. A second later he aggressively pursued the path she had chosen. He slipped his tongue into the eagerness of her mouth. The moment was soft; it was sensual; then suddenly it was a storm unleashing its fury. He felt her heat as she responded with a subtle passion that sent fingers of fire through his body.

She ran her hands across his chest, then down his sides, his taut muscle tone hard to her touch even through the thickness of his heavy shirt. His arms tightened their hold on her. She felt herself being drawn even closer to him. His mouth demanded and she willingly gave. Everything about him told her he was all she could ever want, all she would ever need. She shivered with excitement at the intrusion of his hands beneath her sweater. Her soft moan was swallowed into the depth of his hungry mouth.

His nimble fingers tickled up her back until they reached her bra. His hand moved quickly from side to side, following the band of fabric that spanned her back, then came to rest against her skin. She pulled her mouth away from his just far enough to form the words. Her ragged breathing made it difficult for her to speak. "In front . . . it unhooks in front."

Cody recaptured her mouth with the same fervor that had existed before she broke off the kiss. He consumed her taste, her texture and her essence. Logical thinking had passed out of his easy reach. He wanted her more than he had ever wanted anyone. Was this wrong? He did not know. He slid his hand down her back, caressed the curve of her bottom cheek, then nestled her hips tight against his.

She ruffled her fingers through his hair. His mouth infused her with a heat the likes of which she had never before known. She had felt the hardness of his arousal pressing against her even before he had pulled her body tighter against his. She was certainly not a promiscuous woman, but she was no prude, either. She knew the difference between an inept man who had no idea how to please a woman, a selfish man who did not care about pleasing anyone other than himself and an exciting man who clearly knew every nuance of the fine art of making love. Cody Chandler definitely belonged in the third category.

His hand again slipped up under her sweater. His fingers tickled across the skin covering her rib cage. He wrapped his leg around hers, then rolled her over onto her back. Their mouths remained locked together. The air around them took on a new level of intensity. His hand paused over the lacy fabric covering her breast, then deftly unhooked her bra. A few seconds later he had pushed her bra cups to each side and freed her breasts to his touch. A thud shuddered through his body when he felt her hardened nipple graze his palm. He moaned softly when her ragged breathing thrust her breast fully into his hand.

A similar situation leaped to her mind, a time when his body pressed hers to the floor and his hand scraped against her breast. On that occasion she had lashed out at him in fear. On this occasion she welcomed the warmth of his touch. She ran her fingers down his spine, then grabbed a handful of his shirt and tugged it out of his jeans. She skimmed her fingers up under his shirt and across his bare back, delighting in the tactile definition of his tensed muscles. She fumbled with the buttons on his shirt, unfastening them as quickly as she could.

Cody lifted the hem of her sweater in an effort to pull it over her head. Her bare breasts came fully into his view. His gaze became riveted as they rose and fell with her labored breathing. His breathing was no more under control than hers. His tongue lightly traced a line starting with the notch at the base of her throat and continuing down through the enticing valley between her breasts, all the way to the waist of her jeans. He managed to gasp out some words. "Oh, God. You're gorgeous, Melanie."

He reached his mouth toward her, intent on teasing the delightfully puckered nipple surrounded by the tautly pebbled texture that capped her breast. He stretched his body, inadvertently knocking his leg against her sprained ankle.

"Aaaghh!" Melanie stiffened as her cry of pain filled the air, where only a heartbeat earlier the sounds of passion had dominated.

The sudden outburst startled Cody. He jerked his head back and raised his body up on one elbow. Her pained expression filled his vision. "Melanie?" He gulped in a lungful of air in an effort to force his breathing under control and to stave off the jolt of panic that had materialized when he heard her cry. "What's wrong? Did I hurt you?"

Mel reached toward her wrapped ankle. The throbbing radiated up her leg. She squeezed her eyes shut and bit at her lower lip until the shooting pain had eased. "Whew! The pain has gotten worse. I hope my ankle doesn't feel like this in the morning."

She took a calming breath and at the same time pulled her sweater down to cover herself. The mood was broken. They had started down a path that led to only one destination. Perhaps the interruption came at a fortuitous time, preventing them from succumbing to the heated desires that had controlled their actions. Perhaps they had been prevented from making a costly mistake.

She reached up under her sweater and hooked her bra. Before she could withdraw her hands she felt him briefly cup the underside of her breast, then enclose her hand within his. He held their clasped hands pressed against the warmth of her chest. He felt the rapid thump of her heartbeat.

Cody stared longingly at her kiss-swollen mouth, her lips still moist and inviting, then quickly burrowed his face into the softness of her hair and took several deep breaths. It was more than just his shortness of breath that he needed to bring under control. There was also his emotional involvement and the very real physical arousal straining against the front of his jeans.

He continued to hold her hand while tracing the tip of his finger along the edge of her bra cup. His words were husky, but he was finally able to speak complete sentences without pausing to catch his breath. "I suppose this—" he scratched his finger across the lacy fabric that once again encased the delectable swell of her breast "—tells me that I should dispense with all thoughts that anything more might happen tonight?"

"I think it would be wise to rein in your libido... and mine." She looked into his eyes. The smoky blue glow told of the passion that still burned within him, a passion that she, too, felt very strongly.

He released her hands, then emitted a sigh of resignation. "I guess one of us needed to be sensible and put a stop to things." He slowly rose to his feet. "Besides, the fire needs some attention." He looked back down at her, the hint of a mischievous grin tugging at the corners of his mouth. "It was so hot in here a few minutes ago that I wasn't even aware the flames had almost died out." Even with her face flushed from their amorous encounter, he could still see the crimson tinge of embarrassment cover her cheeks.

Cody turned his efforts to the fireplace. He stacked three more logs on the fire, then stoked it with the iron until it had erupted into a nice blaze. His movements were deliberately slow as he played for enough time to let things cool down between them. He checked his boots to see if they were dry, then turned them around so the other side faced toward the fire.

He seated himself cross-legged on the sleeping bags, next to Melanie. "It was just as well."

His statement confused her. "What was just as well?" His shirt hung open. Her gaze drifted across his bare chest, lingering for a moment on the scratch marks she had inflicted when she first arrived at the ranch. She was pleased that they had healed to the point where they were barely discernible.

He did not answer her question immediately. Instead he pulled her to him, kissed her tenderly on the cheek, then stretched out on the floor, taking her with him. "I'd rather call a halt now than waiting until the last minute when one of us finally had the good sense to realize that unprotected sex with someone you haven't known that long is both dangerous and foolish."

Melanie sat bolt upright. "What?" Both her expression and her voice showed her shock at what he had said.

He sat up and faced her. He cocked his head and eyed her questioningly, as if he was not quite sure he had heard her correctly. "Are you saying you disagree with what I said? In this day and age—"

"No, I don't disagree. I think you're absolutely right. I'm surprised to hear you say it, that's all. I thought most men just assumed the woman was on the pill and that was all—''

He placed his fingertips against her lips to still her words. "Why don't we just agree that we agree and let it go at that? Or—" a soft chuckle intruded onto his words "—did you want to put an end to our second truce by starting an argument about the fact that we concur?"

She held out her hand. "Truce continues?" She could not stop the laugh that filled the air.

He took her hand in his and pressed her palm to his lips. A slight scowl momentarily knitted his brow. He extended a tentative smile. "What's so funny? Was it something I said?"

Her laugh quickly died out. She ran her hand across his chest and tickled her fingers through his chest hair. She felt the beating of his heart, felt his breathing. Her words came out haltingly, the emotion of the situation once again grabbing hold of her. "We were well on our way to making love—" she closed her eyes for a second and took a calming breath "—and, uh, we almost ended up in an argument about the fact that we were getting along."

"Yes . . . we were definitely on our way to making love." His words tickled in her ear. "We've only hit a delay, not a change in plans. I'm right and you know it as well as I do."

"Yes . . . I . . ." There was nothing more to say on the subject. She knew what he said was true.

He pulled her body down to the floor next to him and enfolded her in his arms. They lay side by side in front of the fire, the length of their bodies in tenuous contact. A feeling of closeness surrounded them, a sensual pull that reached out to bind them both physically and emotionally. Neither spoke, nor did they need to. The sounds of the rain on the roof and the burning logs in the fireplace said it all. They drifted into a contented sleep, wrapped in each other's arms, with a promise of what the future held.

Cody finished saddling his horse. Sometime during the night the rain had stopped. The dreary gray of the early-morning sky told of the possibility of more rain. He hoped they would be able to make it back to the ranch house before it started again.

Melanie appeared at the cabin door with the saddlebags in her hands. She held them out toward him. "Here, you take these. I've rolled up the sleeping bags and put them back into the cupboard. I also folded the cots and put them away." A hint of shyness crept into her voice. "Not that we actually used them."

An impish grin pulled at the corners of his mouth as he walked over to her. "Maybe next time." He leaned his face into hers, placed a soft kiss against her lips, then took the saddlebags. "How's the ankle doing? Are you sure it's going to be okay?"

She tested her weight against it. Cody had rewrapped it that morning. It was still sore, but the throbbing pain of the previous night had gone away. "I wouldn't want to try to walk back to the house on it, but it seems fine."

When Cody was satisfied that the last of the embers in the fireplace had been extinguished he closed the door and they started back. They rode double, Cody in front and Melanie behind him with her arms wrapped around his waist and her head resting against his strong back. They rode along mostly in silence. It was not an awkward silence. It was a comfortable feeling of closeness, the same type of closeness they had experienced the previous night.

It was close to noon when they arrived back at the ranch house. Cody dismounted, then turned to help Melanie off the horse. He grasped her at the waist and lowered her to the ground, sliding her along the length of his body before her feet touched down. He held on to her a little longer than need be. He did not want to let go of her. He knew as soon as he did they would both be thrown back into their normal routine, and for Cody that meant a very busy day catching up on the things that had not been done.

"I have to check in with Ross. Roundup starts tomorrow." He brushed some errant strands of hair from her forehead, then placed a quick kiss there. "This place is going to be pretty much deserted for the next few days."

"Are you going out with everyone else?" She did not want him to let go of her. Now that they were back she wished they could have stayed at the cabin, just the two of them, shut away from the rest of the world.

"No, I have too much to do here. In addition to the regular work load, we're also coming up on tax time. Fortunately the computer makes it much easier than it used to be. I can get a fairly accurate report to give to our CPA so he can tackle the IRS forms." He stepped back from her, allowed his gaze to drift across her delicate features, then took the reins in his hand and turned toward the stables. "I'll see you later."

"Yes... see you later." She watched as he led the horse away, then she went to the house. She was in bad need of a shower, but first she would check on her father.

She found Buck sleeping peacefully in his bed. The nurse told her that he had spent a fairly comfortable night. She went on to the kitchen, looking for Edna.

"There you are, sweetie." Edna rushed over to her as she wiped her hands on her apron. "Is everything okay? We were worried about you. I'll swear, Buck was a nervous wreck until Ross came over to tell us he had heard from Cody. I guess the phone signal was pretty bad, but it was enough for Ross to make out that Cody had found you and that the two of you would wait out the night in the trapper's cabin."

Edna noticed the way Melanie was favoring her ankle and limping a little. "You're hurt. Let's have the nurse take a look at that."

"It's nothing, just a sprain. Cody wrapped it for me and it feels a lot better." Melanie pointed toward the coffeepot. "I could sure use some of that and maybe something to eat, too."

"You just sit yourself down right here and I'll have some lunch ready for you in a jiffy."

"I think I'll just grab a cup of that coffee and then go take a shower and clean up first." Melanie gratefully accepted the mug of steaming coffee from Edna and headed for the bathroom.

Cody, too, had opted for some hot coffee in the communications office next to the stables. He also wanted a nice, hot shower, but there was too much work to be done. He spent almost two hours with Ross. This would be the first roundup he had missed since arriving at the ranch. As much as he wanted to participate, this year the business concerns of the ranch precluded it.

When he finished conferring with Ross, he went to check on Moonglow and her new foal. Melanie's Homecoming pranced around the stall on newly steady legs, then sought the security of her mother's proximity. Cody leaned on the railing between the stalls and watched her for a little while. The foal was beautiful, just like the woman for whom she was named...a woman who had been uppermost in his thoughts from that first morning he met her.

Cody left the stables. He had a few additional tasks to take care of, then he needed to bring the computer records up-to-date, juggle a few items and talk to Dennis Sanderson.

Melanie felt much better after taking a shower, washing her hair and putting on some clean clothes. Edna had fixed her something to eat and she had taken it into the parlor. She sat next to her father's bed and watched him as he slept. It had only been a little over twenty-four hours since she had last seen him, yet the continued downhill spiral of his health was startlingly evident.

Buck's head moved slightly, then he opened his eyes. He seemed bewildered until he finally focused on Melanie. His voice may have been weak and raspy, but his face lit up with love and pleasure at the sight of his daughter. "Mel, honey. Are you all right? We were real concerned about you. I was sure relieved when Cody set out in search of you. I knew he'd bring you back nice and safe."

She smiled at him as she straightened his blankets, sat on the edge of the bed, then took his hand in between hers. His icy-cold skin felt uncomfortable, but there was no way she would pull away from his touch. "I'm fine, Daddy. Something spooked my horse and he threw me. I tried to keep from landing on my camera equipment and instead landed on my ankle and it twisted under me. It's going to be okay."

She fussed with his blankets again and adjusted his pillow. "I think I took some really great photographs. Don't know how many of them will be appropriate for a magazine article about modern-day cattle ranching, but if they turn out the way I think there's a chance that I might be able to market some of them to a gallery."

The sound of someone tapping on the window pane grabbed Melanie's attention. She looked up and broke into a big smile. She waved, then leaned over toward her father. "Look, Daddy." She pointed toward the window. She adjusted the head position on the bed so Buck could sit up.

Cody had led Moonglow up onto the porch, with her foal following close by her side. He lifted up Melanie's Homecoming so Buck could get a good view of the mare's first foal.

"Look at her, Daddy. Isn't she beautiful?"

"She sure is, honey." The pride Buck felt could not be hidden, it beamed from his face. "She's beautiful . . . sleek, classic lines."

He closed his eyes for a moment and sank back into the bed. He squeezed Melanie's hand. It was so weak that she was barely able to feel it.

Her voice quavered slightly as she spoke. "Can I get anything for you, Daddy? Do you need anything?"

His words were barely above a whisper. "No . . . nothing. I think I just need to rest a little while." He opened his eyes and looked up at Melanie. "Good night, honey. I'll see you in the morning." Again the faint squeezing of her hand, then he closed his eyes.

She readjusted his bed, then sat next to him, watching his shallow breathing until she was sure he had fallen asleep. She looked up at the window. Cody was no longer on the porch. Apparently he had taken the mare and her foal back to their stall. She continued to sit by her father's bed as he slept.

Cody stared at the monitor screen while talking to Dennis Sanderson on the phone. He had been at the computer for the past two hours, but found that he had to talk to the attorney before he could continue with his work. Cody's needs could not wait until Dennis returned from his business trip to New York.

"We're out of time, Dennis. Both certificates of deposit matured yesterday. I had the funds put into the main account. As far as the financial aspects of the situation are concerned, we can do it either way. What I need from you is a legal opinion about how to handle the two-hundred-thousand-dollar transfer so it won't raise any red flags. The last thing we need right now is someone calling for an audit, especially the bank."

Melanie paused at the office door. She saw Cody seated in front of the computer with the phone receiver to his ear. She had been surprised at how quickly he had eaten his dinner, then disappeared, saying he had some office work to catch up on. She had stayed in the kitchen to help Edna with the dinner dishes, then lingered over coffee while they talked. She caught only the tail end of Cody's conversation.

Cody listened to the response, then made appropriate changes in the computer. "Okay, that takes care of it." Cody exited the program and turned off the computer. "When are you going to be back in your office? We should get together for lunch. Give me a call as soon as you return from New York." He replaced the receiver in the cradle and swiveled around in the chair.

He spotted Melanie standing in the doorway. He had not been aware of her presence. "I didn't hear you come up. How long have you been there?" He rose from the chair and crossed the room.

"Only a few seconds." She indicated the computer with a gesture of her hand. "How's the work coming along?" She did not know what he was talking about, but it certainly sounded like big finance rather than cattle business.

"All done for the night." He leaned against the doorjamb, his body almost touching hers but not quite. "What about you? Anything special you need to do yet tonight?"

The conversation quickly slipped into a personal mood as the sound of the words became more intimate, even if their meaning did not. "Nothing special. I thought I might work on my magazine article. Jeff wanted to see it as soon as possible." His nearness definitely caused little ripples of excitement.

He nuzzled the side of her neck and slipped one arm around her waist. "Who's Jeff?"

She closed her eyes, allowing the pull of his masculinity to latch on to her senses. "He's my agent."

He pulled her body against his and threaded his fingers through her hair. "He's just a business associate?" After what had almost transpired between them the night before he had assumed she was unencumbered as far as personal relationships were concerned. The thought had not occurred to him that she might already be involved with someone.

"He's also my friend." The subtle warmth spread throughout her body. "But, yes . . . it's business."

"Your article—" he flicked the tip of his tongue against her earlobe, then kissed her softly behind the ear "—can it wait until tomorrow morning?"

"I suppose it could." She found it more difficult to breathe at that moment than a mere sixty seconds earlier. "Why do you ask?"

"My room has a nice fireplace and a bottle of good wine. I know it's not an isolated log cabin, but I thought we could build a fire and uncork that bottle." He did not wait for her to answer. He guided her down the hallway toward the suite he occupied.

Nine

Melanie leaned back against a large floor pillow on the thick throw rug and sipped from her glass of wine. "This is an excellent Merlot. I would have thought beer would be more suitable to ranch life." She took another sip as she looked around the room.

"Oh?" Cody tilted his head and raised an eyebrow. "Is that some sort of stereotype you've assigned to anyone who lives on a ranch?"

"No, that's not what I meant." She felt a hint of embarrassment tinge her cheeks. "It's just what I remember from growing up here. Daddy always had cold beer in the stable and that's what the ranch hands would drink at the end of a hot day."

He allowed a slight chuckle. "Well, that's true. Sometimes a cold beer tastes real good at the end of a hot, dusty day. But I also happen to enjoy good wine."

She surveyed her surroundings again—the antique pieces; several unique throw rugs on top of the wall-to-wall carpeting; oil paintings; and some small bronze sculptures of western figures. "I guess this room is more suited to wine than beer." She remembered the guest-room suite from her childhood, only now it looked quite different. The furniture, the decorations, the accessories—they were all a radically different style from the rest of the house. "The only thing that seems to fit in with a ranch are these bronze sculptures. They're excellent reproductions of Remington's work. I don't remember any of these furnishings. Did my father refurnish these rooms?"

"No, when Buck and I decided I needed to move into the main house I had some of my belongings shipped out from New York." He replaced the fireplace poker, picked up his glass from the mantel and seated himself next to her on the floor. He started to correct her, but changed his mind. They weren't reproductions; they were authentic Remington bronzes.

She looked at him quizzically. "I thought you moved from New York a long time ago. You said you'd been here about eight years."

"I moved, but almost all my belongings are still there."

She looked around the room again, taking in everything with a critical eye. The furnishings were not only tasteful, they were also very expensive. Odd, she thought, that he would have kept all these things in storage for such a long time, especially in light of his comments to her. He had certainly alluded to the fact that he had no intention of ever returning to New York to live.

He interrupted her thoughts when he clinked the edge of his glass against hers. "Why don't we propose a toast?"

The magnetic pull of his gaze drank her in just as surely as she drank in the wine. She held up her glass. "What should we drink to?"

His voice took on a husky quality, a sound that seemed to blend with the seductive atmosphere that surrounded them. "Let's drink to us, to tonight and to what the future holds."

The air could not have been more electrified if there had been a lightning storm raging around them. They each took a sip of their wine, as if to seal their commitment to the true meaning of the toast. Cody reached for her glass and set it on the end table along with his. He took her hand, pressed her palm to his lips and captured the glow of the fireplace reflected in her eyes. "I believe we were getting to know each other a little better. Perhaps we could continue where we left off last night." He pulled her to him, enfolded her in his arms and held her body close to his.

All the passions that had existed the night before burst into flame again. Melanie caressed his shoulders, then stroked the length of his back. She felt his tensed muscles beneath the fabric of his shirt. She also felt his warm breath against the side of her neck and her cheek. She sought his mouth, eager for the excitement of his kiss. She found everything she was searching for as the texture of his tongue met hers. The words of his toast rang in her ears. Exactly what did the future hold? Could she be content living on the ranch? She knew if that future included Cody Chandler, then she would be happy no matter where she lived.

Melanie was not the only one with thoughts of the future. For Cody they were thoughts that he was not quite ready to face. He was willing to admit that his attraction to Melanie Winslow was far more than the physical sensations of touching her and kissing her. But beyond that? He had allowed himself to hold out hopes for the future with a specific woman once before and it had been a disaster. Was he willing to put himself through that type of emotional up-heaval again? He was not sure. Or maybe he was sure but was not ready to openly admit it.

The wine was forgotten, the fireplace faded into obscurity and the rest of the world ceased to be. Nothing existed for Melanie and Cody other than the ever-strengthening tie that bound them on all levels.

He slowly rolled her to the floor, cupped her face in his hands and repositioned his mouth against hers. She tasted of fine red wine mixed with an earthy sensuality. It was a deadly combination that threatened to become highly addictive. At that precise moment Cody was more than willing to become hooked for life.

He brushed the side of her neck with his lips, then tasted the base of her throat. He unfastened the top button of her blouse, then the next and the next, kissing each newly exposed patch of skin as it was revealed until the last button had given way. He traced the edge of the lace bra cup that covered the swell of her breast. His words floated across her slightly parted lips. "You're very beautiful . . . and very desirable." His voice was as seductive as his manner.

Their lips met, their tongues meshed, then the heated passions that had been simmering just below the surface exploded with a force that shocked both of them—a force that barely acknowledged the constraints of order and control.

Sweet anticipation filled her consciousness. She tugged his shirttail out of his jeans. Then, starting at the bottom and working her way up to the collar, she slipped each button through the buttonhole in much the same way he had unbuttoned her blouse. Their mouths clung, their lips nibbling and their tongues twining as their heated passions caused their actions to cross over from the smooth to the almost frantic.

He struggled to his feet, pulling her up with him. Pieces of clothing quickly fell away. The sound of their breathing filled the air. She placed a trembling hand against his hard chest, the feel of his bare skin exciting her senses. She watched the heated desire in his eyes, felt the sensual titillation of his touch as he cupped the fullness of her breasts in his hands.

The flames created flickering shadows that danced across the swell of her perfectly formed breasts. The sight and feel of her tautly puckered nipples sent shivers of delight darting through him, his memory suddenly filled with the all-too-brief moment at the cabin. She was exquisite, the most delectable woman he had ever met.

His lips tickled across her throat, nibbling seductively at the curve between her neck and shoulder. Mel closed her eyes and allowed the exhilaration to fill every niche of her body. His touch was magic; his fingers left incendiary trails every place they came in contact with her skin. His caress was gentle and at the same time insistent. He slipped his arms around her and ran his hands across the roundness of her bottom.

She caressed the tensed muscles in his back, splaying her fingers to touch as much of him as possible. Her breasts pressed into his chest as she reveled in the feel of his hands sliding across her bare bottom. She placed several soft kisses and little nibbles across his hard chest. She felt his strong heartbeat. The noticeable increase in his breathing matched her own.

Cody sank to his knees—his hands enclosing the rounded globes of her bottom, his mouth teasing the silkiness of her flesh. He captured one of her puckered nipples in his mouth, suckling gently at first, then with increased fervor. He released the delicate treat so that he could suckle the other nipple. He tickled his tongue across the texture of the puckered flesh, then enclosed it in his mouth, her soft moans of delight spurring him on.

Melanie ran her fingers through his thick hair, then wrapped her arms around his head, holding him tightly against her breasts. He was slowly, sensually, deliciously propelling her toward the ultimate rhapsody—every step of the journey something to be savored and enjoyed to the fullest. They had all night; there was no reason to rush. The heat from the fireplace slowly gave way to the heat building within her and building between them.

The glow from the flames reached out into the darkened room and highlighted the soft curve of her breast, her round bottom, the smooth line of her thigh, the sinewy strength of his arm where it circled her slim waist, the tautly drawn muscles in his back. His ardor increased as he became more aggressive in his actions. Both her nipples stood out hard, the wetness glistening in the light. His tongue teased the underside of each breast, then trailed lightly down her stomach to her navel.

She moaned as the hard tremor of excitement surged through her. Her legs felt weak. She was thankful he was holding her up; otherwise she feared she would collapse. Her titillation increased with the knowledge that they were going to make love on the soft, thick throw rug and pillows in front of the fireplace—capturing the essence of their heated desires as they almost had the previous night. Her fingers dug into his broad shoulders as he trailed hot kisses across her abdomen. An involuntary tightening of her muscles and forward thrust of her hips drove her body harder against his.

As his mouth touched the dark, downy softness nestled between her trembling thighs she gasped, emitted little whimpers of delight, then felt herself sinking to the floor in total surrender. He cradled her body in his arms, gently lowering her the rest of the way. His mouth teased, tasted and explored her textures, until she felt the convulsions begin deep inside and spread throughout her body.

He quickly moved to recapture her nipple in his hungry mouth, while at the same time capturing the heat of her womanhood in his hand, then slipping a finger between the folds of her femininity. She wanted to touch him, to caress his fully aroused manhood, to share the total pleasure he unselfishly provided to her. She felt his hardness pressing against her thigh. His hand continued to stimulate her passions, continued to prolong the explosive convulsions still tugging at her nerve endings.

Melanie gasped for air as the convulsions slowly subsided. She felt his firm muscle tone as her fingers trailed across his hard, flat belly. She reached for his arousal and heard his quick intake of breath as she touched him. His hardness sparked her already inflamed senses. She stroked him in a seductive manner as he greedily captured her other nipple in his mouth. Her body was on fire. She wanted more of him—much more. She wrapped her leg around his and bit at her lower lip as he again ignited her passions to a fever pitch.

Cody was not sure how much longer he could wait. His senses burned for her, more than for anyone else in his entire life. The heat of her response, her unbridled passion, was even more addictive than he had originally realized. He craved more and more. He wanted to give her pleasure as much as he wanted to take it. He reached for the end table, pulled out the drawer and fumbled inside until he located the packet. He quickly opened it and rolled the condom into place. He recaptured her mouth, twined his fingers in her hair, then parted her thighs with his knee.

She welcomed his mouth, aggressively sought out the feel of his tongue meshing with hers. She again caressed his shoulders and back; only this time there was an added sense of urgency as he moved his body over hers. She opened herself to his probing need.

Neither of them had spoken a word. Each was so totally enveloped in the intense emotions governing their actions that words were not only unnecessary, they had become impossible. The swirling heat of their combined passions filled their every breath.

Slowly, ever so slowly, he penetrated her moist heat. A soft moan of intense pleasure escaped his throat. He established an unhurried, smooth rhythm as he skillfully guided her again toward ultimate pleasure.

She had never before experienced the depth of fire or the height of passion he imparted to her. Every fiber of her existence burned with her desire for more of him. She felt wanton, totally uninhibited, as she urged him into a faster rhythm. She clung tightly to him, her legs and arms wrapped around his body, as she again slipped over the edge into a swirling cloud of euphoria. Melanie experienced the most powerful, most exquisite sensations of her life. Cody was, without a doubt, the most skillful and exciting lover she had ever known.

She wanted to cry out as the waves of ecstasy crashed through her body, carrying her to some plane of existence never before visited by mere mortals. She was unable to speak—she opened her mouth, but no sound came out. Her last conscious thought centered on his hardness deep inside her, the heat of his body as it covered hers. She felt his body stiffen. She gave herself totally to the awe and wonder of the powerful sensations.

Cody's senses throbbed with the intensity of his passions. He had never met anyone who set him on fire the way Melanie did, who made him totally lose control of any and all reality other than their two bodies and souls combined into one. His pace quickened; his ardor boiled over as he gave one last, deep thrust. He shuddered as hard spasms wracked his body. He buried his face in her hair and held her tightly until the shuddering spasms ceased.

He felt drained but at the same time knew an excitement and lightness of soul he had never before experienced. He twined his fingers in Mel's hair, pausing every few seconds to kiss her cheek or forehead, while he forced his ragged breathing under control. He wanted to tell her of his feelings, of the emotions that welled inside him whenever he looked at her or heard her voice. But he knew he could not . . . at least not yet. He could not quite bring himself to again expose that most vulnerable place deep inside him to the same type of emotional upheaval he had experienced in New York. To do so would be a big step, one that truly frightened him.

They lay quietly for several minutes, their bodies still entangled. The sheen of perspiration covering their skin glistened in the light from the fireplace. He finally raised the upper half of his body, resting his weight on his elbows. He tenderly and lovingly brushed back several loose strands of her hair from where they clung to her damp cheek, then captured her mouth with a gentle kiss. The fury of their passions had been tamed, at least for the moment, leaving only a soft calm in the wake.

Cody slowly rolled over onto his back, pausing a moment to take a couple of deep breaths. He leaned over and placed a soft kiss on her forehead. "I'll be right back."

Melanie watched him as he walked across the room toward the bathroom, his stride smooth and athletic. She closed her eyes and laid her head back on one of the throw pillows. She felt the warmth of the fire on her skin and the heat from their lovemaking deep inside her. She heard him return, felt him lie down next to her.

Cody pulled her over on top of him with his arms wrapped tightly around her body, one hand caressing her shoulders and the other tickling seductively across her bare bottom. He felt her shiver. He held her tighter, twined his fingers in her hair and kissed her forehead.

Melanie placed a light kiss on his damp chest, then ran the tip of her finger along the outline of his upper lip. The intensity of the still-simmering ardor in his smoky blue eyes burned into her soul.

They continued to lie on the soft carpeting, the flames dancing provocatively across the logs in the fireplace. They spoke very little, relishing the closeness that bound them. Melanie had never been as content as she was at that moment. She snuggled her body closer to his, resting her head against his chest. The sound of his strong, steady heartbeat lulled her into a blissful sleep.

Cody listened to Melanie's slow, even breathing. He found it difficult to verbally express his innermost emotions and feelings. He tried to maintain an orderly and controlled life. Love, however, was neither orderly nor controlled. He glanced toward the fireplace. The flames had almost died out and the room had taken on a slight chill. He carefully untangled their bodies, not wanting to wake her, then gently scooped her into his arms and carried her into the bedroom. He flashed momentarily on the first time their bodies had come in contact, when he had pinned her to the living-room floor on that early morning that now seemed like such a long time ago. He felt as if he had known her forever.

Mel snuggled in the security of his embrace and reached her arms around Cody's neck as he placed her on the large bed. She looked at him through sleepy eyes and smiled dreamily, then rested her head against the pillow. She was not sure whether she had been dreaming, or for that matter was still dreaming, or whether all the magic had been real. She closed her eyes as she felt his weight press down next to her body.

Cody sank into the warmth of the bed. He embraced her, pulled her to him and held her tightly against his body. His voice was soft and loving. "You're very beautiful—not only to look at and to touch, but to be with, to share with." His lips brushed across her face—her cheeks, her forehead, the tip of her nose. He pulled a blanket up over them, then closed his eyes, holding her body in his embrace, pressing it close to his. The enormity of the situation and its meaning filled him with joy to the point of almost overwhelming him.

Cody awoke with a start. He was in bed alone. The bright morning sun shone around the edges of the drawn drapes. He looked at the clock. It was already seven. He had not slept that late in years. He reached to the place next to him, the place where Melanie had slept with her body snuggled against his. The pillow still contained the impression of her head; the warmth of her body clung to the sheets. He glanced toward the bathroom. The door was open and the light was off.

Cody quickly showered and dressed, then went in search of Melanie. She was primary in his mind and in his actions, even more so than taking care of his job. He rationalized his actions by telling himself that if he were sick in bed things would still get done.

He grabbed a mug of coffee from the kitchen, then located Melanie in the parlor, sitting next to her father's bed. He paused in the doorway and watched for a moment as she sipped from her coffee cup. Every few seconds she would reach out and touch Buck's arm or hand. Buck rested quietly, apparently sleeping.

Cody came up behind Melanie and placed a soft kiss on her nape. He whispered in her ear, not wanting to disturb Buck's sleep. "I must have really been out of it. I wasn't even aware of you getting out of bed. I reached over for you and you weren't there. Have you been up very long?"

She had not heard him enter the room. The sound of his voice sent little tremors through her body. She twisted around in her chair until she could see him. His hair was still wet from the shower. His nearness sent the same type of excitement surging through her body as she had experienced the previous night before they had actually made love. She, too, whispered her words. "I haven't been awake that long. I wanted to check on Daddy and didn't want to wake you."

"Too bad you didn't." A hint of a teasing grin tugged at the corners of his mouth, followed by a slightly lecherous chuckle. "I dreamed about the two of us running away together."

She felt his lips on her neck again. Running away together? Exactly what had he meant? The joy she felt bubbled up inside her. Had she heard him correctly? Could he possibly have meant . . .

"What would you think about running away to the barn?" He nuzzled her cheek. "That favorite spot of yours up in the loft?" It was not exactly what his dream had been. But, then, he had not meant to say anything about it at all. He had only added the bit about the barn and the loft to mask his true feelings—feelings he was having a difficult time dealing with.

The bubbles of joy burst before they could rise to the surface. She had allowed her own hopes and dreams to control her thoughts.

Cody had been so intent on covering his slip that he was oblivious to her disappointment. "How's Buck doing? Has he been awake since you've been out here?" He brushed his lips against her cheek, then grabbed her hand and pulled her up from the chair and into his arms.

"No, but the nurse said he had spent a peaceful—" Any and all thoughts flew from her mind as she willingly allowed herself to be folded into his embrace. A second later his mouth was on hers, infusing her with all the heat that had existed between them the night before. She reached her arms around his neck as he pulled her tighter against his body, a touching of planes and contours that they had discovered fit together perfectly.

A soft moan interrupted their rapidly escalating ardor. Buck stirred, then slowly opened his eyes. Cody immediately released Melanie, who rushed to her father's bedside.

"Good morning, Daddy. Did you sleep well?" She adjusted his pillow and straightened his blankets.

"Melanie, honey..."

Talking was obviously a real effort for him. She had to strain to hear everything he said.

"What time is it? I must have nodded off there for a minute."

"It's morning, Daddy." She felt the tears well to the brims of her eyes. He seemed to be fading so fast. Every time she talked to him he was more and more confused. The nurse had explained that it was primarily due to the increased dosage of the pain medication. What the nurse had not said, what she did not need to say, was that the end was very near.

Melanie did her best to blink away her tears and put on a brave smile. "I was about to have some breakfast. May I bring you something to eat or some coffee? Maybe some orange juice?"

"Nothing for me, honey." Buck managed a weak smile. "Maybe I'll have a little something later on. You go on now. Don't worry about me. I'll be just fine. That nice, uh..." His brow wrinkled with confusion as he turned a questioning look toward his daughter. "What's her name? That nice nurse who sits with me?"

Buck focused on Cody, as if just noticing that he was in the room. "Cody? Is that you?"

"Sure is, Buck." Cody stepped closer to his bed. "How are you feeling today?"

Another ten minutes of conversation was all the energy Buck had. Cody assured him that everything was running smoothly—most of the ranch hands had started out on the roundup.

Buck drifted into a light sleep. Melanie watched him for a moment. Cody stayed with her, his arm reassuringly around her shoulder. Buck was his best friend. He knew the end was imminent and it filled him with a tremendous sense of loss. He also knew that Melanie would need someone she could lean on and he was that someone. He gave her shoulder a supportive hug.

Cody had a lot of work to do. After making sure Melanie was all right, he left the house to start on his busy day. The time passed quickly. He would occasionally catch a glimpse of her at a window and a couple of times she stepped out onto the porch for a few minutes. He would wave and continue with his work load, at least he continued with the physical motions. His mind, however, was totally absorbed with deeply personal thoughts.

Making love with Melanie had resulted in a truly profound revelation for him. Perhaps he could once again allow himself to be vulnerable, to show his emotions, to give his heart to a very special woman. Maybe he could love again without fear. That special woman who had set free those very real fears was Melanie Winslow.

The timing, however, was rotten. There were business matters to take care of, things that needed to be handled in a pragmatic manner without the complication of his personal feelings. There were numerous transactions that had to be finalized prior to Buck's death. Cody had done his part; hopefully Dennis Sanderson would complete his side of the arrangements in time. The thought sounded harsh, but it was true. He would have to try to explain it all to Melanie later, but not now.

Melanie stayed in the parlor with her father. He spent most of the time sleeping, occasionally waking for a few minutes, then nodding off again. She could not stop her thoughts from drifting toward what would happen after her father was gone. She supposed everything would go to her as his only heir. She had never given any thought to one day owning the ranch. She had always considered her father invincible, a strong man who would live forever.

She did not know anything about running a ranch, but Cody did. What would happen to their relationship? Employer and employee? Lovers? Would he even want to stay on as her employee? Should she just sell everything? Whatever she decided, it had to be something that would allow Cody to feel free to be with her without constraints caused by business ties.

The sudden activity of the nurse jarred Melanie out of her thoughts. Panic welled inside her, rooting her to the chair so that she was unable to move. All she could do was stare while the sickening lump formed in the pit of her stomach.

Cody left the stables and went back to the house. As soon as he stepped inside the front door he heard the commotion. A cold tremor shook through his body. He rushed to the parlor.

The nurse was huddled over Buck, Edna was next to her and Melanie sat in the chair on the other side of the bed— her face an ashen mask. Cody quickly crossed the room to Buck's bedside. He swallowed hard. This was it; he could feel it in his bones. He looked to Edna, who discreetly nodded, confirming his thoughts.

"Melanie, honey..."

Buck's voice was a breathless whisper; she had to lean close to hear what he was saying. "Yes, Daddy. I'm here." She took his hand in hers. It was icy cold and exhibited no strength at all.

"Mel... I love you, honey. I'm so happy you came home. Now I can join your mother and know that everything's okay. Don't you worry about anything here. Cody will take care of things. He knows exactly what to do."

"Now, Daddy..." She forced out the words while making a valiant attempt to suppress her sobs. "Don't talk that way. You'll be here for a long time yet."

Buck closed his eyes as his head sank back into the pillow. Melanie brought her hands to her mouth. Her entire body trembled; her throat went dry and tried to close.

"Cody..." It was obvious that Buck was making a supreme effort to force out his words.

"Yes, Buck. What do you need?" Cody had to lean in so close to make out what his friend was saying that his ear was almost against Buck's mouth.

"I've heard you and Melanie argue. And I've seen the way you look at her when you think no one's watching. I've seen the way she looks at you, too. Her mother and I used to have some dandies. Virginia had an indomitable spirit... one of the things I loved about her. She stood up for what she wanted and what she believed. Melanie is the same way, always has been. Remember, making up sometimes makes the argument worthwhile." Buck took several breaths before he continued. "Promise me, Cody. Promise you'll take care of Melanie for me. See that she's okay, that she's happy...."

Cody straightened up and placed his hand on Buck's chest. There was one last, faint gasp, then nothing. He glanced over at Melanie. The haunted expression that covered her face tugged at his heartstrings every bit as much as the realization that he had just felt his friend take his final breath. He looked up at the nurse, who silently acknowledged that his assessment was correct. His gaze returned to Buck. He squeezed his friend's shoulder, even though he knew Buck was beyond the ability to feel the gesture. "I'll do my very best, Buck. I promise you I will."

Melanie had not heard what her father said to Cody, but a cold shiver moved through her body just the same. She looked to Cody for confirmation of what she instinctively knew, that her father had just died. She wrapped her fingers around the locket that graced her neck, then closed her eyes. A moment later she felt Cody's arm around her shoulder.

Cody pulled Melanie to him, held her for a moment, then spoke softly. "Come on. I'll walk you to your room."

He tried to guide her toward the door, but she refused to move. She stared at her father for a moment, then reached out and touched his cheek. Her words were whispered through sobs. "Goodbye, Daddy. I love you."

Ten

Cody stood on the porch and watched as the last of the taillights disappeared down the long driveway leading to the main road. Arrangements had been made months ago. It took only one phone call to Doc Gerrard to set everything in motion. The funeral would be a very simple graveside service, then Buck would be laid to rest next to Virginia. Buck had specifically stated that he did not want a lot of fuss, did not want people to feel obligated to interrupt their workday on his account.

The previous six months had been extremely complex. There had been lots of arrangements to make, lots of legal maneuvers. Cody had spent many hours with Dennis Sanderson. Everything had gone along smoothly and efficiently until Buck took over the handling of the business affairs via computer. It had cost Cody many additional hours to undo the mistakes Buck had made, errors due in part to his lack of computer accounting experience and also to his increased disorientation, caused by his medication.

And then things had been complicated even more by the sudden and unexpected appearance of Melanie Winslow. Did she have any thoughts about the future of the ranch? Any plans she might have formulated but kept to herself?

Cody stepped off the porch into the breeze that had turned from gentle to brisk within the space of less than an hour. He shoved his hands into his jacket pockets and hunched his shoulders against the crisp night air. Even though he had mentally prepared himself for this moment, he still felt a profound loss at the passing of his friend.

He wandered toward the stables. Now the picture had changed and so had the rules. He leaned against the railing and watched Moonglow and her foal. Melanie's Homecoming stood strong and steady on her long legs, her coloring matching the mare's nearly luminous gray hue. Cody entered the stall, stroked Moonglow's long neck, then turned his attention to the foal. He ran his hand down her neck and along her flank. He tested her legs, then administered an affectionate stroke to the foal's nose.

Next he went to the communications office. He needed to contact Ross Andrews out on the range and give him the news. He reached Ross via the cellular phone. "And be sure the men understand that I don't anticipate any changes in the way things are being run. Everyone's job is secure. Buck was also specific about not wanting the work schedule interrupted. Naturally, anyone wanting to come in to attend the funeral services may do so, but make sure people understand it's okay if they don't."

Cody felt at a real loss. He knew he should be in the office, preparing the paperwork for the bank. Dennis Sanderson would be reading the will following the funeral. Cody already knew what it contained. He was also aware of

a couple of changes that should have been made but had not
been rewritten.

His thoughts turned to Melanie. She had professed a desire to be alone, saying she wanted to start going through her
father's things and pack up his clothes. He debated whether
to disclose the unusual provisions of her father's will or
leave it to the official reading by the attorney. He was not at
all sure how she was going to respond. It was a tough decision, but he finally opted for waiting. He did want to check
on her, though, make sure she was all right.

Melanie had folded all her father's clothes and packed
them in cardboard boxes. She had been surprised at the
sparseness of his wardrobe. Other than the one suit Cody
had retrieved from the closet for the funeral, his clothing
consisted mostly of a few pairs of jeans and some work
shirts. She remembered the suit as the one he had worn to
her mother's funeral. It would be much too big for him now,
but it was the only suit he owned. It was obvious that her
father had led a very isolated life for the past ten years as far
as any social engagements were concerned.

How strange things were; what a totally unexpected turn
of events the past week had produced. She sat in the rocking chair, the one she remembered her mother always sitting in, and held the sweater her father had been wearing the
first morning when he entered the kitchen while she and
Cody were fighting. It was well worn, apparently a particular favorite of his. She held it close to her heart, her
mother's locket pressed between the sweater and her skin.
She closed her eyes as the tears trickled down her cheeks.

"Is there something I can do to help you?"

Cody's voice was soft, his words cloaked in genuine concern. Melanie opened her eyes and slowly turned her head
in his direction. She immediately rose to her feet and placed
the folded sweater in the cardboard box with the other shirts

and sweaters. "I was just packing the last of Daddy's clothes."

She seemed flustered, as if she were embarrassed at being caught with her grief showing. Cody took her hand in his and laced their fingers together. "You don't have to do this if you don't want to. I can pack up his things for you."

"Oh, Cody..." She wrapped her arms around his waist. "Why...he was always so strong, so..." She did not know exactly what she wanted to say. All she knew at that moment was that she desperately needed someone to hold on to, someone to tell her that everything was going to be all right.

"I'm sorry you didn't have more time with him." He threaded his fingers through her hair and cradled her head against his shoulder. "Buck was a wonderful man and a very good friend. My best friend." He had not allowed himself any personal reflections, preferring instead to maintain a strong persona. He had learned to keep his innermost thoughts and feelings to himself. "He was closer to me than my own father." It was a small admission, but one that cut through to his innermost reality. He held her tightly, providing her the comfort she sought and understanding her need. "I know he loved you very much. Seeing you again was the thing he wanted most."

Buck was not the only one who loved her. Cody had wrestled with the dilemma several times and each time the answer was the same. What he felt was not a momentary infatuation, it was not a temporary emotional attachment and it was not simple lust. It was love. There was no other word for it. What he did not know was what to do about it. His thoughts jerked back to the present when Melanie pulled out of his embrace.

She reached into a dresser drawer and withdrew a small box. She handed it to Cody. "Here, I would like for you to have this. It's Daddy's pocket watch. From as far back as I can remember, he always wore it."

Cody opened the box and took out the gold watch. Buck had been wearing it the first time they'd met. He replaced it in the box and put it in his pocket. His words were soft and filled with the emotion of the moment. "Thank you. I'll always treasure it."

She tried to muster a confident attitude. "I'm not sure what happens next. I suppose the logical thing for me to do is acquaint myself with the ranch's business dealings. I don't know anything about the financial status of my father's holdings. I don't really know anything about running a ranch, either. I imagine I'm going to have several hard decisions to make over the next few weeks so I'd better familiarize myself with things."

She looked up at him, concern covering her face as she furrowed her brow. "That doesn't sound crass, does it? I mean, it doesn't sound like I'm trying to pry into his money..." She paused for a moment, her eyes downcast and her voice soft as she finished her sentence. "I hope it doesn't sound like I'm assuming that I automatically inherit everything just because I'm his daughter—"

She captured Cody's gaze again, a sense of urgency in her voice. "I don't want you to think that all I care about is money and material possessions. That the only reason I'm here is to try to take something. That's not true at all." She felt her anxiety rising to an uncomfortable level. "That's not what people here think, is it? They don't think I showed up just to take what I could get, do they? I make a comfortable enough living. My car, my photographic equipment and my computer are all paid for. That's all I have. It's all I really need."

"I know, Melanie." He framed her face with his hands and placed a loving kiss on her lips. "I know." Things were certainly not cut and dried. He wanted to wait until everything was settled. After all the loose ends were tied up, then maybe he and Melanie could sit down and discuss the future. But until then he would have to take one step at a time and hope he did not stumble and fall.

"Is there anything else you need to do in here?" He wanted to change the subject. "If not, you look as if you could use a breather." He caressed her shoulders, then drew her to him. He held her for a moment, resting his cheek against the top of her head. His voice was soothing as he drew her in emotionally as well as physically. "I know it's been a very trying time for you. You don't need to worry about throwing yourself headlong into the ranch business. Everything is under control and running smoothly."

He nestled her body against his, allowing his hand to slide down her back and seductively graze the curve of her bottom. "If you decide to stay here, you can ease your way in as you become comfortable with it." *If you decide to stay*...he was not even sure why he had said that. Of course she would stay—she had to stay.

He kissed the side of her neck, then whispered in her ear. "Why don't we have a glass of wine, then first thing tomorrow morning we can start out fresh?"

"Mmm...that sounds nice." She closed her eyes and gave herself over to the warm feeling that suffused her body. Cody Chandler was very persuasive. She had concluded that he was probably capable of charming a snake out of its skin if he wanted to. He had certainly charmed her. She knew it was more than just his smooth, practiced manner. For the past ten years she had been like a ship without a rudder or an anchor. She had a successful career but seemed to be drifting, without any sense of home or belonging.

He had a stability, a commanding presence and an inner strength that made her feel safe and secure when she was with him. This stability was not something she had been consciously seeking, but it was one of the things she loved about him. She did not even flinch at her realization. Love was precisely what she meant. She was not sure exactly how things would be worked out, but she knew it was right. She allowed him to lead her from her father's bedroom.

The first streaks of early-morning gray seeped in around the edges of the drapes. Cody had been awake for almost an hour. He watched Melanie as she slept in his arms. Once again they had made love with a heated intensity that had not diminished from their first time together.

As much as he hated leaving the warmth of his bed and the closeness of Melanie, he had work to do and it was better done when there was no one around to interrupt him. He quietly slipped out of bed, showered and dressed, then went to the office.

He quickly and efficiently made necessary changes in the accounts, transferred funds, faxed signed authorizations and sent reports to Dennis Sanderson via the computer's modem. He leaned back in his chair and stared at the report on the monitor screen. It was the financial statement that Dennis would give to Melanie when he read Buck's will. Cody was about to sign off the computer, when he was surprised by Melanie's voice, her words still thick with sleep.

"You're certainly hard at work for so early in the morning. When did you get up?"

He swiveled around in his chair until he faced her. Her feet were bare and her hair still tousled in a just-got-out-of-bed manner. She had pulled on one of his T-shirts, the hem dropping down her sleek thighs halfway to her knees. She looked very enticing—wild, uninhibited, sexy and totally desirable. He held his hand out toward her, motioning for her to join him.

"Come here." The huskiness that immediately attached itself to his words matched the shortness of breath that caught him by surprise. He grabbed her hand as soon as she came within reach and pulled her down into his lap. He slipped his hand inside the T-shirt and ran it up her bare back. "Mmm..." He nuzzled her neck and playfully nipped at her earlobe. "Let's go back to bed. I think I'd like to have you for breakfast." He ran his fingertip along the swell of her breast. "I'm sure I could find all kinds of tasty things to nibble on."

"That's a powerfully tempting offer..." Her words trailed off as the information on the computer screen caught her attention. "What's that? Is it something I should be looking at? Something to do with the ranch's business records?"

He swiveled the chair around until he faced the computer again. He was not sure how to answer her. "Well, it's some of the information that goes with Buck's will." He felt her body stiffen as she pulled back from him.

A strange sensation shivered through her body at the same time as the unwanted thought popped into her head. She rose from his lap and straightened the T-shirt. She could not keep the trace of suspicion from creeping into her voice. "Why do you have access to it before the will is even read? Where did you get it?"

He took a calming breath. It was a delicate situation and he wanted to make sure he handled it properly. "I have it because it came from me." He noticed her startled expression, followed by the quick frown that wrinkled her brow. "What I meant to say is that I'm the one who put the information together for Dennis Sanderson. I'm the ranch's business manager in addition to foreman, so part of my job is to handle the financial matters." He was not happy with the nervousness that jittered inside him. "I was checking it to make sure everything was in order before transmitting the statements to Dennis.''

Her unabashed surprise clung to each and every word. ''Do you mean that you are the one who has control of my father's finances?''

''Yes . . . I told you I had a degree in finance. You knew I was taking care of ranch business on the computer. What did you think I was doing?'' He reached out for her, attempted to pull her back down into his lap. A barely audible sigh escaped his throat. ''Unfortunately the business side of dying has to be handled immediately. It can't wait until the emotional side is under control.''

Melanie sidestepped his attempt. She ran her fingers through her mussed hair. ''I, uh, I think I'd better take a shower and get dressed.'' She took a couple of steps toward the door, then turned back toward him. Her words were somewhat tentative; she was not confident of her ground. ''I'm sure there are several details that need to be tended to—'' A wave of sorrow washed through her. She tucked it away. This was neither the time nor the place. He was right about taking care of the business of dying, no matter how painful. ''With regard to the funeral arrangements.''

Cody rose from the chair and quickly covered the short distance separating them. ''There's nothing, Mel. All the arrangements were made months ago. Buck took care—'' Cody felt his iron grip on his emotions beginning to slip. He took a steadying breath. ''Buck took care of everything personally. The only task remaining was the phone call to the doctor when it was—''

He walked over to the window and stared out at the mountains in the distance. There were too many things happening that required his attention. He could not allow himself the privilege of indulging his grief. He needed to steel himself against the sense of loss that he knew would last for a long time to come. His voice was almost a monotone. "Buck calmly and rationally picked out his own casket, decided there should only be a small and brief graveside service and made it very clear that he did not want a bunch of people notified and did not want a eulogy delivered." He folded his arms across his chest and continued to stare out the window. "He said all he wanted was to be laid to rest next to Virginia."

He sensed Melanie behind him, then felt her arms slide around his waist and her head come to rest against his back. His voice became reflective, matching his thoughts and words. "Buck loved this view, especially this time of year—the green pasture dotted with wildflowers and the snow-capped Rockies in the background." He tilted his head backward until it touched hers and placed his hands on top of her hands. It was a moment of comfortable closeness.

He was trying to show a solid strength, but Melanie could hear otherwise in his voice. She could tell that his grief was very real. He obviously hurt, but apparently felt he did not have anyone he could turn to for comfort. The beginnings of a confrontation over the computer information and Cody's role in the business affairs of the ranch were shoved aside. The confrontation would have to wait until another time.

Cody took her hand and led her around until he was able to enfold her in his embrace. They stood together in silence, wrapped in each other's arms, staring out the window. It was a time of closeness and emotional sharing that surpassed any physical desires. They lingered in silence for a while longer.

Melanie slowly untangled herself from his arms. "I'd better get dressed." She gave his hand a squeeze. "Are you sure there isn't something I should be doing?"

Cody returned her hand squeeze and extended a comforting smile. "No, everything has already been done. The burial will be tomorrow morning at nine o'clock."

Melanie left the office and went to her room. Her mind kept vacillating between the emotional toll of the events and her not yet wholly formulated suspicions about the possible manipulation of the financial records by Cody and even the likely assistance of Dennis Sanderson. It was a troubling thought, one she chose not to dwell on.

She reached for the phone and called Jeff. "I've done some preliminary photography on the modern-day-cattle-ranch article and have been working on a brief outline, but I'm afraid it'll be a couple of weeks before I can get anything to you."

She listened to what her agent said, then responded. "I'm sorry, Jeff, but that's the way it has to be. My father died yesterday. The funeral is tomorrow, followed by the reading of the will. After that there're going to be numerous business matters that must be dealt with immediately." As much as she had tried not to dwell on it, the ranch's financial matters and Cody's involvement refused to stray very far from the forefront of her mind.

She concluded her conversation with Jeff, picked up a couple of her cameras and headed outside. As she passed the office she spied Cody sitting at the computer. He seemed to be almost trancelike as he just stared at the monitor screen without moving. Perhaps later, when Cody was away from the house, she would be able to access the files and see for herself what was there.

She wandered toward the stables, paying more attention to the ground immediately in front of her than looking ahead to where she was going. She could not shake her suspicions about Cody and his handling of her father's business dealings. If she truly loved Cody, then she should trust him. But if she did not trust him did that mean she really did not love him? She thought she loved him, but how could she be sure? The thought both perplexed and scared her.

She entered the stable and went to Moonglow's stall. The mare and her foal both swiveled their ears in her direction, then turned their heads toward her as if to acknowledge their acceptance of her presence in their space. The morning sun streamed in through the opened doors, filling the interior with the golden illumination of a beautiful day. She opened the gate and stepped into the stall. The foal sought the safety of her mother's proximity. Mel gently stroked Moonglow's neck and flank, then reached into her camera bag and produced a plastic bag containing carrots and apple wedges.

She held several pieces in her open palm and offered them to the mare. Moonglow accepted the offering, then allowed Mel to click off several good photographs of mother and daughter.

One more moment of sadness heaped itself on top of all the others. Melanie's Homecoming—her father had named the foal after her. Ten years had been wasted, ten years she could have spent getting to know a man she only thought she had known. And eight years wasted that could have been spent with Cody Chandler.

Moonglow nudged Melanie's shoulder as her way of insisting on more carrots and apples. Melanie stroked the soft velvet of the mare's nose, then gave out more treats. She snapped one last picture of the foal, picked up her camera bag and left the stables.

After skirting the corral, Melanie walked out into the meadow behind the barn. She breathed deeply. The green grass smelled of spring; the wildflowers provided a riot of color. She looked out toward the mountains, lifting her hand to shade her eyes from the sun. It still bothered her, still pricked at her consciousness. What was Cody doing

with her father's finances? It tore at her insides, this battle
between her suspicions and her love.

She found a large rock, set her camera bag on it, then
settled herself in, using the rock as a backrest. She had so
many decisions to make. The will had not even been read yet
and already her father's property and finances had her life
in turmoil. Should she stay on the ranch and try to run it
herself? Should she sell everything and go back to Los Angeles? Perhaps she was taking more for granted than she
should.

She had assumed that being her father's only direct heir
meant everything would be left to her, but maybe that was
too presumptuous of her. After all, they had been es-
tranged for ten years. Her father certainly had every right to
dispose of his property in any manner he chose. She was
afraid to give any conscious consideration to the possibility
that she and Cody could run the ranch together . . . as partners.

Melanie picked a wildflower and twirled the stem between her finger and thumb. The still-vivid heat of Cody's
lovemaking warmed her insides and filled her with the love
she felt for him. She had a lot to think about. Slowly she
pulled the petals from the flower. "He loves me . . . he loves
me not . . . he loves me . . ."

Cody had watched from the office window as she walked
out into the meadow. Everything that could be done before
the reading of the will had been done. At least things were
in an acceptable and manageable state of affairs. The rest of
the changes would have to be made later, when he could sit
down with Melanie and explain to her why things had been
set up the way they were and why the provisions of the will
read the way they did.

He hoped Melanie would understand and accept what
Buck had wanted. He hoped Melanie would want the same

thing. But regardless of how things turned out between Melanie and him, he would see to it that Buck's wishes were carried out. If anyone had told him a month ago that when the time came his loyalties might end up doing battle with his desires, he would have said the person was crazy.

He hoped it would not come down to having to make a choice. He could not betray Buck's dying request, but he feared he might never recover if he ended up losing Melanie.

One way or the other, it would all be over in one more day.

Eleven

Melanie sat on the edge of her bed and looked around her bedroom, studying the possessions of her youth. Everything had a different feel than when she had first entered the room after a ten-year absence. Now she looked at her early amateurish attempts at photography with the knowledge that it was her father who had gone shopping for her first camera. She picked up the photograph of her mother from the nightstand and her hand involuntarily went to the locket around her neck. She missed her mother so much, and now, thanks to her own obstinacy, she'd barely had a chance to know her father before he, too, was gone from her life forever.

She left her bedroom and wandered down the hall to her father's bedroom. With the funeral the next morning, a very difficult chapter of her life would be closed. She felt as if her very existence had been turned inside out. Sinking into the security of her mother's rocking chair, Melanie leaned her head back and closed her eyes as they filled with tears. She again curled her fingers around the gold locket, seeking the calm and comfort it seemed to provide her.

She had no idea what the future would bring. Again her thoughts turned to the man who made her tremble with excitement, the man who stirred the type of feelings in her she had never before experienced—the man she had definitely fallen in love with. Was it possible that she might be opening a new chapter to her life? A chapter she and Cody could share together?

"There you are." Cody's voice was soft, yet contained a hint of concern. He had been looking for her. When he did not find her in the kitchen or living room, he had gone out to the barn on the off chance that she might be in the hayloft. It had not occurred to him to look in Buck's bedroom. It was only as he was walking down the hall that he heard the faint creaking sounds of the rocking chair against the hardwood floor. He had paused at the door and peered into the darkened room.

Melanie slowly opened her eyes. She had sensed his presence, knew he was there even before he spoke. She allowed a tiny sigh of despair as she turned her head toward him. Her voice was barely above a whisper. "I was just sitting here thinking. Wondering what the future would bring."

He knelt next to her and ran his fingertips across the well-worn denim covering her thigh. He, too, had been wondering about the future. He did not want her to leave the ranch. From a purely selfish standpoint, he did not want to have to choose between following her to God knows where or staying in the only place he ever truly felt happy, but without her.

He tried to calm his trepidation as he rose to his feet. He took her hand and pulled her up from the chair. "Come on, you can't sit here in the dark all by yourself." Still clasping her hand in his, he led her from her father's bedroom. She offered no resistance as they continued down the hall to his suite of rooms.

She totally gave herself over to his control. She did not want to be responsible for making decisions, at least not that night. She knew the next day was going to be very difficult for her, but for tonight she wanted only to rid her mind of all the troubling thoughts. It was more than just the funeral, the reading of the will and the business matters that would require immediate attention. What troubled her most of all was the uncertainty that surrounded her true relationship with Cody Chandler and their future together...if any.

The moment his lips touched hers all thoughts ceased to exist, all except one. Cody Chandler was now the most important person in her life.

Their clothes quickly fell away, then they sank into the softness of Cody's bed. She clung to him as he took her hardened nipple into his mouth, suckled for a moment, then moved to the other nipple.

Her body burned with her hunger, a hunger that screamed out to be satisfied. She caressed his muscled torso, sliding her hand down his hard rippled belly until she reached his fully aroused manhood. The feel of his arousal sent tingles through her fingertips. She stroked him seductively, taking pleasure in the feel of his hardness.

He moaned softly as he lay back, resting his head on the pillow and taking delight in her sensuous touch. He closed his eyes and allowed the sensation to envelop him. His chest heaved with his ragged breathing—a situation not helped by the little kisses she scattered across his shoulder and chest, then down his belly.

She lowered her head, provocatively teasing him with her tongue. His texture, his taste, his masculinity sent tremors darting through her body. She heard his quick intake of breath, followed by the animal growl of intense rapture that clawed its way out of his throat as he jerked his head back into the pillow.

He tried to gain some control over his highly stimulated senses. She was rapidly driving him into oblivion. He gasped out the words, "Melanie...I..." He was unable to talk, to formulate any words. He reached down to her, pulling her up until her body stretched out on top of his. He devoured her mouth in a frenzied burst.

Cody firmly grasped her hips and lifted, then lowered her onto his hardness. His fervor increased tenfold as the searing heat of her womanhood tightly encased his rigid masculinity. He thrust his hips upward, reaching as far into her as he could.

She emitted little whimpers of delight when his arousal penetrated to the farthest depths of her desires. Her body slumped forward against his as he enfolded her in his loving embrace. She rocked her hips back and forth, creating a delicious buildup of intense sensations deep within. He was allowing her to control the rhythm, to adjust for her needs. He was, without a doubt, the most giving and generous lover she had ever known.

The convulsions rippled through her, then the searing explosion of her release flooded hot and hard inside her body. She gasped for breath, allowing him to take control. He carefully rolled her over onto her back, maintaining the tangible connection between them. He again captured her mouth as his hips coaxed her into his smooth rhythm.

He felt her muscles contract around his manhood, sending tremors of exhilaration coursing through his body. She excited him as no one else ever had and he had difficulty maintaining even a modicum of composure. He wanted this to last forever yet at the same time he wanted to consume her in a blinding flash of electrifying tumult.

His thrusting increased in both tempo and force as his own euphoria teetered on the brink. With one final plunge he buried himself deep inside her, holding her tightly in his embrace. The spasms shuddered through his body, his words came out in a breathless rush. "Mel ... you're so ... Oh, Melanie...I..." He stopped himself just in time—just a breath away from telling her he loved her.

The hard spasms that rocked through his body propelled her to an intoxicating level of ecstasy usually reserved for the privileged few who resided on the top of Mt. Olympus, in the heady realm beyond the scope of mere mortals.

They clung tightly to each other, arms and legs entangled, as the wildfire that ignited their passions slowly came under control. Even after a calm settled over them, they remained tangled together. Neither wanted to let go, neither wanted to disturb the opalescent aura that surrounded them. They held each other, they reveled in the emotional closeness that existed between them.

He smoothed her hair away from her damp cheek and forehead, then placed a soft kiss on her lips. She snuggled into the warmth of his embrace. They exchanged the quiet murmurings of lovers basking in the warm afterglow of their intense lovemaking. He held her body close to his, gently stroking the silkiness of her skin. Finally, they drifted into a contented sleep.

Melanie stood on the front porch, staring at the gathering of dark clouds on the western horizon. Another spring storm was poised just over the crest of the Rockies, ready to roll down the eastern slopes and across the foothills, bringing more rain to the ranch.

The funeral would be in two hours and she was not dressed yet. She did not seem to be able to force herself into a quickened pace. She had packed hurriedly when she left Los Angeles, and certainly not with a funeral in mind. She tugged at the bottom of her sweatshirt and brushed at her jeans. The only thing she had with her that was even close to appropriate was a charcoal gray blouse and a pair of black slacks. She stepped off the porch and wandered aimlessly toward the meadow on the other side of the barn.

Cody watched her from the kitchen window. Even though their lovemaking had been every bit as intense as the previous times, Mel had still spent a restless night. She constantly tossed and turned. Every time he woke up he found her staring up through the dark toward the ceiling. He had held her close, tried to comfort her, but she seemed to sleep only in snatches.

"Do you need me for anything, Cody?" Edna's words broke into his thoughts. "If not, I think I'll get ready for the service."

"You go ahead, Edna." Cody put his arm around her shoulder and gave it an affectionate squeeze, then kissed her cheek. "You've been a real treasure. I appreciate all the little extras you did to make Buck's last few months more comfortable. He may not have said so, but I know Buck appreciated it, too." He gave her another squeeze.

"What's going to happen now, Cody?"

He could hear the uncertainty in her voice, feel the tension in her body. "I'm not sure. The reading of the will is at one o'clock this afternoon. It shouldn't take long. You don't need to worry about anything, Edna. There'll always be a job for you—" his voice trailed off, as if he had lost his train of thought for a moment "—if not on the ranch, then certainly with me."

"Oh, Cody. . ." She heaved a heavy sigh of sorrow. "I'm going to miss him so much. He was such a fine man."

"I know. I'm going to miss him, too." He gave her shoulder another squeeze before releasing her.

Half an hour later Cody stepped out on the porch, dressed in a dark-gray suit, light-gray shirt and a maroon-and-gray patterned tie. He spotted Melanie on the porch swing. She sat perfectly still, her fingers wrapped tightly around the stems of a small bouquet of wildflowers. He could not see her eyes behind her dark glasses, but she appeared to be staring out toward the mountains.

"It's time. Are you ready?"

Melanie had not heard him walk out onto the porch. His voice startled her. She jumped at the feel of his hand on her shoulder. She looked up at him, then removed her sunglasses.

As soon as he touched her he felt the tension in her muscles. When she removed her dark glasses he could see the red puffiness of her eyes. She looked down at the bouquet she held, then raised the flowers to her nose, inhaling the delicate fragrance. "Yes, I'm ready."

Cody removed his suit jacket, hung it on the valet rack, then loosened his tie and unfastened the top button on his shirt. The funeral had been just the type of simple service Buck had wanted. Now it was over and he was once again with his beloved Virginia.

Melanie had not said a single word on the ride back from the cemetery and had gone straight to her room as soon as they arrived home. Cody had tried to comfort her, but she had been unresponsive and seemed to be very much drawn into herself. He sat on the edge of his bed, then leaned back on his elbows. Dennis Sanderson would be there in three hours for the reading of the will. The worst part of the day was yet to come.

Cody forced himself into action. There was still ranch work to be done. Quickly he changed into jeans, denim shirt and boots, grabbed his hat and gloves from the top of the dresser, and paused by Melanie's bedroom on his way out of the house. He hesitated a moment, then knocked softly on the door. "Mel, are you in there?"

"Yes." She opened the door. "Come in... please." Her reply was immediate and positive, her smile friendly, but the stress in her voice and apprehension in her eyes told a different story.

Cody dropped his work gloves inside his hat and tossed the hat on top of the desk. He wrapped his arms around Melanie and held her close to him. He wanted so much to comfort her, to ease her obvious pain, but he was not sure exactly what to say. He knew what he wanted to say. He wanted to tell her he loved her. He never thought he would say that to another woman, not ever again. He loved her very much and did not want to lose her. In just a little while it would all be over; everything would be out in the open.

Melanie nestled into Cody's embrace, taking from him the strength he willingly provided. There was more going on inside her than just the emotional toll of her father's funeral. In a very short amount of time everything would be settled legally. Then there would only remain the clarification of her relationship with Cody. She had no idea how finalizing her father's estate would affect things. She loved Cody. That was the only thing she knew for sure.

Cody kissed her tenderly on the forehead. "Will you be okay for a little while? I have some work to do before Dennis gets here."

"Sure, I'll be fine. You go ahead. I think I may take a little nap. I didn't get too much sleep last night." She looked up into his eyes and offered a bit of a shy smile. "I hope I didn't keep you awake with all my tossing and turning. I guess I just had too many things on my mind to go to sleep, too many problems that need to be resolved."

He pulled her body tight against his in an almost panicky type of gesture. His words were soft, barely above a whisper. "Oh, Mel. You're...you're very important to me. Please believe that. Whatever happens, whatever direction the future takes..."

Had she heard him correctly? They had exchanged thoughts and beliefs on a variety of subjects, even delved into personal aspects of their lives, but this was the first time either of them had dared to verbally share some of those innermost feelings. She tried not to read too much into his words, tried not to make them mean what she hoped they did. She could not, however, stop her increased heartbeat and the excitement that tried to force itself to the forefront.

She returned the added intensity of his embrace. "I...I feel very close to you, too."

On the surface it was a totally unnecessary exchange of words, considering the fact that they had already made love several times, but to delve deeper into the reality uncovered something else. Each was unsure and somewhat uncomfortable about exactly where the personal murmurings were headed and what might be brought out in the open. This thing called love—for Melanie it was brand-new, uncharted territory. For Cody it was a painful road he had traveled once and was not sure about traveling again. He traced her jaw with his fingertip, then cupped her chin in his hand. The words that followed were almost inaudible. "You're more than just important to me—you're all-important." He leaned down and placed a loving kiss on her lips. He searched the depths of her eyes as he tried to put his thoughts and feelings into words. "Melanie, I—" He recaptured her mouth with a searing intensity. It was the only way he could stop himself from telling her that he loved her very much.

He released her from his embrace and took a couple of steps backward. "I'd better go. Dennis will be here soon and I have lots of things to do. I'll. . ." He snatched his gloves from inside the hat and pulled them on, then settled his Stetson comfortably on his head before turning toward the door. "I'll see you in a bit." He quickly left her bedroom, closing the door behind him.

An uncontrollable shiver of apprehension sliced through Melanie's body, setting all her nerve endings on alert. She did not understand Cody's sudden change in attitude and mood. One moment he was kissing her senseless and the next moment he didn't seem to be able to get away from her fast enough. She tried to dismiss the feeling by attributing it to her lack of sleep and the emotional drain of the funeral. She tried, but she knew it was not so. While his kiss had been every bit as passionate as she knew him to be, it also tasted of something else . . . something sad and disturbing.

Melanie went to the kitchen to get a glass of ice tea. On the way back to her bedroom she stopped in the office, seated herself in front of the computer and turned it on. She gave the appropriate commands and was rewarded with a listing of what was available on the hard disk.

She pulled up the accounting records and began reading them from the monitor screen. What she saw shocked and confused her. It appeared that two certificates of deposit, each for six months in duration and in the amount of one hundred thousand dollars, had matured just a few days ago. The money had been deposited in the ranch's account, then the day before her father died it had been electronically transferred out to a New York bank account. *This must be*

the money she had heard Cody discussing on the tele-
phone. The thing that disturbed Melanie the most was that
her father had been incapable of authorizing any such
transaction.

Cody had prepared the financial reports—she had seen
him working on them. Her brow knitted as she bit at her
lower lip. Maybe things would become clear when the attorney arrived, but right now they were a muddled mass of
confusion. She shut down the computer and left the house.

Melanie wandered out to the stables to see how the new
foal was doing. She leaned against the railing, watching
Moonglow and Melanie's Homecoming until she heard the
car in the driveway. She looked out the stable door and saw
Dennis Sanderson stepping from his car. She had met him
at the funeral and had also renewed her acquaintance with
his father, Henry Sanderson. She took a deep breath and
slowly expelled it. The reading of the will was all that remained. She took another deep breath and returned to the
house.

She was the last one to arrive in the living room, where
Dennis, Cody, Edna and Ross Andrews had already con-
gregated. She seated herself on the couch. The nervousness
churned in the pit of her stomach. She glanced at Cody, who
seemed surprisingly ill at ease.

"Well, now that everyone is here we can proceed." Dennis opened his briefcase and withdrew a legal document. "If
there aren't any objections, I'll dispense with the reading of
the legalese that covers the 'being of sound mind and body'
and all the other 'to wit' and 'whereas' clauses. Buck has
named Cody Chandler as executor of his will. These are the
bequests of Buckminster Franklin Winslow, as set down in
his last will and testament six months ago and witnessed by
Richard Cody Chandler III."

The third? Richard Cody Chandler III? Melanie had not realized Cody was his middle name. And *the third?* He had told her his father was in banking, but it suddenly seemed as if Cody Chandler was much more than he had let on...much more. She returned her attention to what Dennis was saying.

"To Edna Powers, my housekeeper and my friend, I leave twenty thousand dollars in cash and the directive that she has a job here if she desires for as long as the parameters of this will are in effect."

Edna dabbed at her eyes with a tissue. "Buck was such a fine gentleman, but that's much too extravagant of him."

Cody slid over next to her on the couch and put his arm around her shoulder. "Buck thought the world of you, Edna. He wanted to make sure you were properly taken care of."

Dennis continued. "To Ross Andrews I leave five thousand dollars in cash and my heartfelt thanks for his hard work and loyalty."

"That's right nice of Buck." Ross turned his attention to Melanie. "Your daddy was a good man, Miss Winslow, an honest and kind man, who was generous to a fault."

"Thank you, Ross."

Ross stood up and turned toward the door. "I know this probably ain't fittin', but if you'll excuse me I need to be gettin' back to work. There's lots to be done." He tipped the brim of his hat to Melanie, nodded his acknowledgment to the others, then left.

Dennis Sanderson continued, "There's one more bequest. It was a little tricky to put it in order, but it was Buck's exact instructions. This is for you, Melanie."

The attorney's words startled Melanie. Only one more bequest and it was for her? She found it difficult to believe that her father had not left anything to Cody.

Dennis continued, "At the time of the writing of this will, Buck had no idea where you were and had not heard from you since you left home. He knew he only had a few months to live and would probably not see you again. He set up a holding company, sort of a trust, with Cody as the administrator. Buck has directed that Cody have sole control over the assets as follows."

Melanie squirmed uncomfortably in her chair. Her anxiety expanded until it filled every available corner of her consciousness as she listened to what Dennis Sanderson was saying.

"Eighty-five percent of the ranch plus one hundred percent of Buck's other holdings, consisting of various stocks and bonds, with the exception of the bequests to Edna and Ross, are under the control of this holding company as of two weeks ago. Buck's instructions provided that everything remain in the holding company for a period of ten years from the time of his death. If, during that time, you were located, then your inheritance would still remain in the holding company and under Cody's control for the duration of the ten years.

"At the end of that ten-year period the holding company would be dissolved and the inheritance would be turned over to you. If after making every reasonable effort you still had not been located by that time, then the holding company would be dissolved and sole ownership of everything would revert to Cody. The final provision states that you may not sell your eighty-five-percent ownership of the ranch while it is part of the holding company without Cody's authorization, and that once the holding company has been dissolved the ranch property cannot be sold off in pieces—only one hundred percent of it can be sold as one transaction. This means that your eighty-five percent cannot be sold without Cody's agreement to sell his fifteen-percent ownership along with it.''

Melanie sat in stunned silence. Had she heard correctly? She glanced at Cody, then turned her attention to Dennis. She was not sure how to word her question. "Uh, excuse me, Dennis . . . am I understanding this correctly? Cody already owns fifteen percent of the ranch? Owned it prior to my father's death? And now he also controls the remaining eighty-five percent, even though I inherit it?''

"That's right, Melanie. Buck gave fifteen percent of the ranch to Cody as a gift.'' Dennis handed her a large, sealed envelope with a small envelope paper-clipped to it. "I realize things might appear a bit unorthodox, but those were Buck's very specific instructions. This is a copy of Buck's will, his financial statements, the accounting structure for the holding company and a personal message for you from Buck. I want you to look over the papers at your earliest convenience.''

He closed his briefcase and prepared to leave. "If you have any questions, please feel free to give me a call. I should be back in my office in an hour or so.'' He shook hands with Melanie, then turned his attention to Cody. "I'll talk to you tomorrow.'' The two men shook hands and Dennis left.

Melanie watched from the window as Dennis's car disappeared down the long driveway. Edna had already returned to the kitchen. Only Cody and Melanie remained in the living room.

Twelve

Cody had seen the shock on Melanie's face and heard the edge to her voice when she questioned Dennis. But he didn't know what was going through her mind. As he stood behind her and placed his hands on her shoulders, her tightly knotted muscles felt hard to his touch. He felt her flinch when he touched her, then she shrugged out of his grasp. He could not stop the stab of pain caused by her rejection.

Melanie did not know what to think. Cody had witnessed the will. He knew exactly what it contained. He owned fifteen percent of the ranch and had control over her eighty-five percent for the next ten years, yet he had not mentioned a word of it to her. She felt numb inside. She felt betrayed, and the biggest hurt of all was that it was by the man she loved.

Once again living on the ranch has brought her heartache—with one very significant exception. She had found a father she had never really known. A caring man who had never stopped loving her, regardless of how she had behaved toward him. Their time together may have consisted of only a few days, but it was a loving memory she would carry with her for the rest of her life. She wrapped her fingers around the locket that adorned her neck. No matter what happened, no one could take that away from her. Not even the painful realization of Cody's betrayal could erase that loving memory.

"Melanie..." An intense jab of emotional pain shot through Cody when she moved a couple of steps away without turning to face him or acknowledge that he was talking to her.

He took a calming breath, grabbed her shoulders firmly in both hands and turned her around to face him. He did not like the way she had clenched her jaw, or the unidentifiable glint in her eyes. "Listen to me, Melanie. We have things to talk about. I don't know what your expectations were, but I do know that some of what you just heard came as a complete surprise to you. I wanted to tell you what was in the will, but I was ethically bound to wait—"

"Ethically? You speak of ethics? How can you even say that?" She fought to keep the hurt out of her voice. "I thought there was something special between us, that maybe—"

"There *is* something special between us, Mel, something very special. I—" He drew her into his embrace and held her tightly as he took a steadying breath. She did not push away from him, but she did not return his embrace, either. It had to be said and it had to be said right now. To put it off until a more opportune time would only make things worse, if that was possible... and assuming that such a thing as an opportune time even existed.

Cody took another calming breath, then continued. "I don't have any type of flowery speech prepared. Maybe I'm not even saying it the way I should or the way you would want to hear it, but I love you, Melanie. I love you so very much."

She looked up at him. Had he only been playing games with her? Was this yet another game? How was it possible for what should have been the happiest moment of her life to end up being the saddest? "You have no idea how much I've wanted to hear those words from you, how much I've wanted to say them to you." A wave of sorrow rippled through her body. "Only now it's too late. There's no longer any reason for you to say them."

She could not prevent the anguish from entering her voice or the overwhelming pain from tingeing her words as she pushed away from him. "You don't need to pretend with me any longer. You've already accomplished what you set out to do and you did it very cleverly. You now have control, though not complete ownership, over my father's ranch. It's official—a done deal."

His insides knotted to the point of being physically painful. He knew she would be surprised, even a little confused, by the parameters of the will . . . but this? "Melanie, please—"

She deftly sidestepped his attempt to hold her. "I understand my father establishing some type of a holding company to keep the ranch in trust while trying to locate me. But the rest of it? By getting a dying man to give you fifteen percent of the ranch you eliminated the problem of it being part of the will." She finished with what she felt was the most damaging evidence of all. "And what about the two hundred thousand dollars?"

She turned to face him squarely, prepared for the guilt she imagined would show on his face. What she found, instead, was an overpowering agony that shone in the depths of his blue eyes, so much so that it shocked her into stunned silence for a moment. It seemed so genuine. It almost subdued her own anguish.

Cody could not have been more crushed if she had accused him of murder. He had finally worked up the courage to tell her he loved her and in return she had accused him of wrongdoing with her father's property. His heightened level of stress showed in his voice, along with his total bewilderment. "You...you're accusing me of acting improperly? Of being dishonest? Of somehow swindling my best friend?" A hint of disappointment and sadness crept into his voice. "I thought you would have known me better than that by now."

His words were shockingly brutal. She had not intended to... She was not sure what she had meant. Cody did not allow her any time to put her thoughts in order or to clarify her comments.

His face was an impassive mask, with his jaw set in a hard line. "Well, I guess that about says it all." He put on his hat, pulling the brim low over his forehead in a manner that obscured her view of his eyes. "You make things very difficult for me. Buck's last words were for me to look out after you, to see that you were happy."

He walked toward the door, paused and slowly turned toward her. "How do I do that, Miss Winslow?"

She heard the pain in his words. It tugged at her heart. Where had it all gone wrong?

"What is it that will make you happy? What do I need to do to honor my best friend's dying request?" He opened the door. "When you figure it out, let Dennis know. I'll check with him periodically to see what you need. Any paperwork and instructions concerning the ranch can be handled through his office. In the meantime, I'll have my belongings cleared out of the house...out of *your* house by the end of the week." Cody walked out of the room, closing the door behind him.

Melanie watched from the living-room window as he quickly covered the ground between the house and the stables. When he was out of sight, she turned her attention to the large envelope Dennis had given her. She stared at it, but did not open it. She was not sure what to do. The only thing she was sure about was that the man she loved had just walked out the door... and possibly out of her life.

She went to her bedroom, tossed the large envelope on the bed and reached for her jacket. She spotted the small envelope peeking out from underneath the large one. Her father's note... the legal paperwork could wait, but not her father's note to her. She retrieved the envelope and withdrew the single sheet of paper. The handwriting was very shaky. The note had obviously been written during her father's final days.

Melanie, honey, it's finally all over. I'm at rest now. I know the things in my will may seem a little strange, but I wanted to safeguard against you possibly making a hasty decision about the disposition of the ranch. I want you to keep it, honey, to be able to pass it on to your children. Cody will help you with everything. Please trust his judgment in these matters. I love you, Mel. You made my last few days very happy ones.

She had run from the ranch once before, pushed by her own erroneous assumptions, and it had cost her ten years of not knowing a loving father. Now she was about to cut and run again. When would she learn her lesson? Could she afford, once again, to turn her back and walk out on someone she loved?

She stared at the large, sealed envelope. Maybe there would be something in the financial statements that would explain the two hundred thousand dollars. She reached for the envelope, then paused. No. Her father trusted Cody implicitly and had asked her to do the same. Besides, a relationship without trust does not have a strong foundation and cannot withstand over the long haul. She loved Cody, but if she did not love him enough to trust him and believe that he acted honorably, then a relationship would not stand a chance.

She left her room in search of him. They needed to talk this out before it was too late. She spotted Ross. "Do you know where Cody is? I need to speak to him."

"Well, ma'am. He took off about twenty minutes ago, headed out across the pasture on horseback. Didn't say where he was goin', but looked like he planned to be gone for a couple of days."

"Oh..." She felt the sharp pang of disappointment. "Thank you, Ross." She slowly turned and started back toward the house, then a thought struck her. Could he have gone to the cabin?

She whirled around and called to Ross. "Could you saddle a horse for me?"

"Certainly, Miss Winslow. Proud Warrior is in the corral. Would he be okay or would you rather—"

"That's fine. Thanks." She started back to the house, then broke into a run. She grabbed a saddlebag, packed a few things, then ran back to the stables just as Ross led Proud Warrior out into the yard. She mounted and headed out at a full gallop across the pasture, into the afternoon sun.

Only the last fleeting rays of sunset still colored the sky when Melanie reined Proud Warrior to a halt and sat astride the horse for a moment as she stared at the old trapper's cabin. Cody's horse was in the lean-to. A plume of smoke curled out of the chimney. Lantern light seeped out around the edges of the shuttered window. Her guess had been correct. This is where he had gone. She urged her horse forward.

Cody sat on the floor in front of the fireplace. His entire life had been thrown into turmoil and he did not know what to do about it. In spite of the fact that he had impulsively taken off, he knew he could not permanently run away from the problem. Nor could he casually dismiss his deep feelings of love for Melanie. Regardless of their deteriorated relationship he still had his responsibilities to Buck and to the ranch.

He stared into the flames. Maybe he needed to think about moving on, possibly back to New York. He could administer things long distance. He knew he could not bear to stay in daily contact with Melanie knowing that her every look and thought said she considered him a dishonorable man who had cheated her father.

Sure, he could explain to her that the money transfer was simply the repayment of a personal loan he had made to Buck four years ago. The transaction had been a handshake deal between the two men without the legal paperwork or even a signed IOU. It had been put into certificates of deposit and appeared on the ranch's balance sheet as an asset without showing the money owed to Cody as a liability that would have canceled out the asset.

It had been done as a means of making the ranch's financial position more attractive with regard to securing a large loan for upgrades and new equipment. Dennis and Buck both wanted the money transferred out before Buck's death so that it would not be tied up as part of the estate. That way Melanie would not have any inheritance taxes levied against the money. The time frame in doing that had been very tight due to the decision to wait until the certificates matured rather than converting them early.

What had hurt him the most was her accusation that he had coerced a dying man out of part of the ranch. Buck had given him that fifteen percent a little over three years ago, before the cancer had been diagnosed. Cody had put all the profits from his share into a special account and had never touched the money. Somewhere in the back of his mind he had thought of it as a safety net for Buck in case the ranch fell into serious financial troubles. Buck had discussed the will with him and Cody had made it clear that he did not want any more than he already had.

"That's a very serious look you're sporting there, cowboy. Is something the matter?"

He snapped around in surprise at the sound of Melanie's voice. He had been so absorbed in his thoughts that he had not heard the door open, had not heard her enter the cabin. She looked uncertain, as if unsure of her ground. She also looked beautiful. His heart swelled with the love he felt for her, a love that was still every bit as strong as it had been before everything fell into an abrupt downward spiral.

She quickly continued before Cody had a chance to say anything. "Is it possible that you're upset, albeit justifiably so, over some stupid comments and irrational accusations made by a crass woman who didn't have a clue what she was talking about?" She felt her composure slipping away. "Someone behaving in a regrettable but hopefully forgivable manner?"

She had never been so scared in her life. What if he rejected her apology? It took her a moment to even realize she was holding her breath. It seemed like forever before he spoke, even though it was really only a second or two.

He remained seated on the floor in front of the fireplace. His voice was soft and filled with an unmistakable warmth. He held out his hand toward her. "Come here."

To her great relief he did not seem angry. She went to him, kneeling next to where he sat. She was determined to somehow repair the damage she had done. "Cody—"

He touched his fingertips to her lips to still her words, then cupped her chin in his hand. He leaned his face into hers, but stopped just short of their lips actually touching. "Does this mean you've figured out what it is that will make you happy?"

"Yes . . ." His lips were so close to hers, his nearness so tempting. "I think I've figured it out."

"Good." He brushed his lips across hers. "Tell me . . ." He nibbled at the corners of her mouth. "I can't carry out Buck's last request if I don't know."

She felt the catch in her breathing and her increased need for oxygen. "First, it will make me happy if you forgive me for what I said to you. I am so very sorry, Cody."

"Does this mean you don't want the answers to the concerns you raised?" He eyed her, looking for her reaction to his words.

"I had no right to make those unfounded, wild accusations. My father thought the world of you and it was obvious how much you cared for him. I was way out of line in suggesting that you might have done something to hurt him. You don't have to explain anything to me if you don't want to. My father trusted you . . . and so do I."

He could tell how difficult the words had been for her to say. He could also tell that they came from deep inside her, from a place of honesty. "Of course you're forgiven." He wrapped his arms around her and pulled her into his embrace. "The ranch's records and all financial transactions are totally available to you. I'll be happy to answer any questions you want to ask. Now, what next?"

Her words were hesitant. "I've decided to give the ranch a try." Her manner grew more tentative. "It would make me very happy if we could work together . . . uh . . . as business partners." She was not sure exactly what she was leading up to. She was fully aware of how difficult he could be making this for her, how much her horrible accusations must have hurt him. Instead he was treating her deplorable actions as if they had not even happened.

His lips were close enough to hers that she could feel his words as he spoke. "Is that all? Just business partners?"

Her heart pounded wildly. She barely had enough breath to get out the words. Her insides were doing flip-flops. Dare she say it? "Partners in love ... partners in life?"

The smile tugged at the corners of his mouth, then spread across his face before he could stop it. The joy he felt at that moment was almost more than he could contain. "How about partners *for* life...partners forever? Is that what will make you happy?" He nuzzled his face into her hair. "I know it will make me happy. I love you, Melanie Winslow." He laid her back against the unfolded sleeping bags that covered the plank floor.

The burning wood popped and crackled in the fireplace. She reached her mouth to his, initiating a soft, loving kiss. "I think I started falling in love with you that first morning, when you found me in the hayloft."

He brushed his lips against hers again. "I love you very much."

She traced the tip of her finger across his upper lip. "I sure hope so, cowboy, because I intend for you to marry me."

The teasing grin and soft chuckle were immediate. "Well, if that's what it takes to make you happy..."

The light of the kerosene lantern and the illumination from the fireplace could not compete with the glow of their love.

* * * * *

Who can resist a Texan...or a Calloway?

This September, award-winning author
ANNETTE BROADRICK
returns to Texas, with a brand-new
story about the Calloways...

SONS
→OF←
TEXAS

Rogues and Ranchers

CLINT: The brave leader. Used to keeping secrets.

CADE: The Lone Star Stud. Used to having women fall at his feet...

MATT: The family guardian. Used to handling trouble...

They must discover the identity of the mystery woman with Calloway eyes—and uncover a conspiracy that threatens their family....

Look for **SONS OF TEXAS:** Rogues and Ranchers in September 1996!

Only from Silhouette...where passion lives.

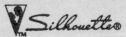

SAVE *up to 50%!*

As seen on TV!
Free Gift Offer

With a Free Gift proof-of-purchase from any Silhouette® book,
you can receive a beautiful cubic zirconia pendant.

This gorgeous marquise-shaped stone is a genuine cubic
zirconia—accented by an 18" gold tone necklace.

(Approximate retail value $19.95)

Send for yours today...
compliments of ▼ *Silhouette*®
™

To receive your free gift, a cubic zirconia pendant, send us one original proof-of-
purchase, photocoples not accepted, from the back of any Silhouette Romance™,
Silhouette Desire®, Silhouette Special Edition®, Silhouette Intimate Moments®
or Silhouette Yours Truly™ title available in August, September or October at your favorite
retail outlet, together with the Free Gift Certificate, plus a check or money order for
$1.65 U.S./$2.15 CAN. (do not send cash) to cover postage and handling, payable
to Silhouette Free Gift Offer. We will send you the specified gift. Allow 6 to 8 weeks for
delivery. Offer good until October 31, 1996 or while quantities last. Offer valid in the
U.S. and Canada only.

Free Gift Certificate

Name: _____

Address: _____

City: _____ State/Province: _____ Zip/Postal Code: _____

Mail this certificate, one proof-of-purchase and a check or money order for postage
and handling to: SILHOUETTE FREE GIFT OFFER 1996. In the U.S.: 3010 Walden
Avenue, P.O. Box 9077, Buffalo NY 14269-9077. In Canada: P.O. Box 613, Fort Erie,
Ontario L2Z 5X3.

FREE GIFT OFFER   084-KMD

ONE PROOF-OF-PURCHASE

To collect your fabulous FREE GIFT, a cubic zirconia pendant, you must include this
original proof-of-purchase for each gift with the properly completed Free Gift Certificate.

084-KMD

You're About to Become a

Privileged Woman

Reap the rewards of fabulous free gifts and
benefits with proofs-of-purchase from
Silhouette and Harlequin books

Pages & Privileges™

It's our way of thanking you for
buying our books at your
favorite retail stores.

PROOF OF PURCHASE

SD-PP164

Offer expires October 31, 1996

Harlequin and Silhouette—
the most privileged readers in the world!

For more information about Harlequin and
Silhouette's PAGES & PRIVILEGES program call the
Pages & Privileges Benefits Desk: 1-503-794-2499

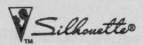

Silhouette®

SD-PP164